DRUG WARS
A NEW DOPE
(A Star Wars Parody)

By

Matthew J. Pallamary

Mystic Ink Publishing

Mystic Ink Publishing
San Diego, CA
www.mysticinkpublishing.com

ISBN 13: 979-8-9884998-2-4 (sc)

Library of Congress Control Number: 2025912026
Mystic Ink Publishing, San Diego, CA

Book Jacket and Page Design: Matthew J. Pallamary/San Diego CA
Cover artwork: Matthew J. Pallamary/San Diego CA
Author's Photograph: Matthew J. Pallamary — Robert DeLaurentis /Santa Barbara CA

This book is dedicated to Poloka Lele.

Long may you fly.

Drug Wars
A New Dope
(A Star Wars Parody)

A long time ago in a cannabis field far, far away…

ONE

Bathing in the warm amber glow of approaching dusk, a young man with dreadlocks who looks younger than his twenty years looked out over a gently swaying field of mature cannabis plants. He opened his slender muscular arms wide, tilted his head back, and stretched out, inhaling the intoxicating perfume of blossoming terpenes wafting to him on a gentle breeze.

A dreamy smile filled his face. He leaned forward to touch his feet and found himself face to face with a large red mushroom with white spots that he recognized from all the fairy tale and fantasy books and pictures he had ever seen.

He glanced up at the rose colored sun sinking low on the horizon then back at the mushroom. His vision flashed and the mushroom looked like it fluttered in a rainbow of flickering colors into the form of a beautiful girl with a cannabis bud for a hairdo. He blinked in disbelief and the image disappeared, leaving the mushroom which now had an orange glow shining from its red and white flecked surface like it was under a spotlight.

Unable to resist its call he plucked it up and rinsed it off with water from his water bottle, then he slowly chewed it up and swallowed it in pieces, washing them down with sips of water. He swallowed the last piece at the moment the sun winked out in an explosive flash of rose colored glory. Another rainbow flicker burst into a spectacular accelerated psychedelic sunset of colors and patterns that played out in the diminishing light, giving way to the beginnings of a starlit sky draped above a vast sea of cannabis.

Bob Marley's song "Weed" echoed through his mind and out into the surrounding heavens which undulated with waves of ripples, shifting patterns, and geometries that danced to the beat of the music before forming into glowing green words floating across the sky, scrolling upward, lifting off into space and disappearing into infinity…

It is a period of drug wars in the galaxy. Rasta Freedom Grower vapeships striking from a hidden underground grow have won their first victory against the evil Corporate Hempire.

During the battle, rasta spies managed to steal plans that hold the secret to the Hempire's ultimate weapon, the DEATH BONG, an armored space station powerful enough to destroy an entire planet with its paraquat ray.

Pursued by the Hempire's crack smokers, Princess Sensimilla races home aboard her vapeship with stolen plans that can save her people, stop Inferior control over the galaxy's cannabis production, and restore the freedom to expand consciousness throughout the galaxy.

The words brighten into an overwhelming flash followed by shifting geometries and connected patterns that dissolve, coalesce, and shrink into a large black disk. A razor thin line of light shimmers along its right side before the slowly spinning multihued planet of Tryptamine emerges from its eclipse. Concentrated colors and patterns move across its surface like active psychedelic storm clouds.

A tiny sleek stylized silver vape pen spacecraft races into view trailing smoke, followed by a massive glass bong shaped Inferior warship replete with polychrome blinking lights, artillery batteries, turret guns, radars, and other offensive and defensive armaments. It fires a colorful plasma laser on the fleeing vape ship eliciting an explosion and more smoke before the smoldering Rasta ship is overtaken by the Inferior battle bong.

TWO

An explosion rocks the rebel vape ship as two dopebots, 2CB and 5MEO struggle through the shaking, bouncing main passageway. 2CB is a short hookah looking roach clip armed tripod that moves on tank tread feet. His face is a mass of cannabis-themed graphic displays that show expressive eyes, eyebrows, mouth, and nose at critical times surrounding a central fixed polychromatic third eye.

5MEO is a slender humanoid dopebot with gay mannerisms and gleaming metallic surfaces that swirl with shifting colors, intensity, and patterns that reflect his thoughts, emotions, and speech. At this moment he speaks with a gay sounding Jamaican patois punctuated by flashing bright red like a walking fire truck and his red carapace intensifies with each word. "Did you hear that? They've shut down the main reactor. We'll be vaporized for sure!"

2CB answers with a series of shifting panicked faces and electronic pot smoking sounds, beeps, and squeals that only 5MEO can understand. Dreadlocked Rasta troopers rush past them and take up positions in the main passageway and the tension mounts as loud metallic footsteps and the screeching of heavy equipment are heard moving around outside the ship.

"There is no escape for the Captain this time..."

A huge smoke billowing blast opens up a hole in the main passageway and a score of fearsome Inferior Crack Smokers make their way into the smoking corridor, then the passageway blazes with plasma fire that ricochets everywhere creating huge psychedelic explosions. Black armored Inferior Crack Smokers with green fan-shaped cannabis leaves on their chests scatter and duck behind storage lockers. Plasma bolts hit several red, gold, and green armored Rasta soldiers who have Rastafari standard bearing lion flags on their chests causing them to scream and stagger through the smoke with smoldering dreads.

An explosion hits near the dopebots and the lanky 5MEO becomes entangled in a mass of dangling wires that spark and pop like different colored Fourth of July fireworks every time he attempts to move, stimulating more intense colors and patterns across his surface. 2CB waddles to his aid.

"Help me!" MEO shrieks. "I think something is melting. This is all your fault! I should have known better than to trust the logic of a half-sized shake burning roach clip…"

2CB counters with a rebuttal of angry facial expressions that end with an electronic fart sound as the battle rages around the two helpless dopebots.

THREE

A shimmering white rainbow-hued wasteland stretches from horizon to horizon. The heat of two huge flowing multicolored suns settles on a lone figure, Dude Dopetoker, a cannabis grower with slender muscular arms who looks younger than his twenty years. His dreadlocks and baggy tie-dyed tunic give him an air of stoned simplicity.

A light wind whips at him as he adjusts several valves on a moisture vaporator, a large battered hi-tech pipe and tank device sticking out of the desert floor. He is aided by a beat up tread dopebot with six roach clip arms and a faded flickering display. The little dopebot is barely functioning and moves with jerky motions.

A bright sparkle in the morning sky catches Dude's eye. He grabs a pair of lidar enhanced electrobinoculars from his belt and stands transfixed studying the heavens, then dashes toward his dented, crudely repaired weedspeeder floating a few feet above the ground. He motions for the tiny dopebot to follow him to the weedspeeder, a flying tractor shaped like a small glass pipe that glows orange in the front bowl compartment when it is energized. "Hurry up! What are you waiting for?"

The dopebot, painted in faded rasta colors scoots around in a tight circle and stops. Smoke pours out of every joint. Dude throws his arms up in disgust and jumps into his weedspeeder, leaving the smoldering dopebot to hum madly amidst a puff of smoke from the back of the weedspeeder.

FOUR

The awesome, seven foot tall Ron Raygun, The Dank Lord Of The Spliff steps into the smoke filled main passageway of the rebel vapeship. Raygun is the right hand of the Hempress Nancy. His face is obscured by flowing dark green robes and a breath mask that looks like the head of a circumcised penis with a large cannabis leaf on the front that sounds like a toke on a joint every time he breathes before speaking in a deep booming voice. His garb stands in contrast to the fascist black armor of the Inferior Crack Smokers. Everyone backs away from the imposing warrior and several of the rasta troops run in panic.

5MEO stands in another smoky hallway, bewildered. 2CB is nowhere in sight. The pitiful screams of doomed rasta soldiers can be heard in the distance. "2CB! 2CB! Where are you?"

A gurgling bong hit sound attracts MEO's attention and he spots little 2CB at the end of the hallway in a smoke filled alcove. A beautiful young girl with a cannabis bud shaped hairdo is kneeling in front of 2CB looking surreal and out of place like a holographic dream half-hidden in smoke. After adjusting the third eye on 2CB's computer face she watches the little dopebot join MEO, then she is gone.

"Where have you been? They're heading in this direction," MEO lisps. "What are we going to do? We'll be sent to the fentanyl mines of Opioid or smashed into pipe screens. Wait, where are you going?"

Twocee scoots past his humanoid friend and races down the sub hallway. MEO chases after him.

The evil Ron Raygun stands among the broken, smoking bodies of the rastas in the vapeship's cockpit corridor and grabs a wounded rasta officer by the neck holding him high above the ground until an Inferior Officer rushes up to him saying, "The information retrieval system has been wiped clean."

Raygun squeezes the neck of the rasta who struggles while his dreads start to smoke. "Where is the data you intercepted? What have you done with those vape cartridges?"

"We intercepted no information!" the Rasta officer chokes out between gasps. "This is a consular ship. Didn't you see our markings? We're on a diplomatic mission…"

Raygun tightened his grip on the Rasta, choking off his words. "Where are those cartridges?"

"Only… only the commander knows…"

"This ship carries the crest of Cannabis. Are any of the royal family on board?"

The rasta cries out as the Dank Lord squeezes his throat harder, causing his dreads to ignite until the soldier goes limp. Raygun tosses the dead rasta against the wall and turns to his crack smoker troops. "Start tearing this ship apart piece by piece until you have those vapes. Find the passengers of this vessel. I want them alive."

The crack smokers snap to attention and raise their hands in a stiff nazi-like salute with their middle fingers extended, speaking in unison, "Just say no!", before scurrying off into sub-hallways.

In another part of the ship 2CB stops before the hatch of an emergency vapepod cartridge and snaps the seal on the main latch. A multicolored warning light flashes and the stubby hookah dopebot works his way into the cramped four man pod.

"Hey!" MEO shouts. "You're not permitted in there. It's restricted. You'll be deactivated for sure."

2CB makes gurgling bong hit sounds, beeps, and whistles at his reluctant friend.

"Mission? What mission? What are you talking about? You've short circuited. I'm not getting in there!"

2CB makes angry beeps, buzzes, and coughing sounds, then his face displays a middle finger ending with an electronic fart sound.

"Don't call me a mindless blunt, you overweight glob of pipe tar…"

A new explosion sends dust and debris through the narrow sub-hallway and flames lick at MEO. After a flurry of agitated electronic bong gurgles and coughing sounds from Twocee, the lanky dopebot jumps into the vapepod with him. "I'm going to regret this."

The vapepod carrying the two terrified dopebots speeds away from the stricken rebel spacecraft on the main view screen of the Inferior Star Destroyer cockpit.

"There goes another one," the pilot says, pointing.

"Hold your fire," an officer orders. "There are no life forms. It must have short-circuited. Don't waste your plasma."

The slow swirling rainbow-hued mass of Tryptamine seems to engulf the tiny vapepod containing the two dopebots and the starships grow smaller as the pod descends toward the planet.

FIVE

The beautiful girl with the cannabis bud hairdo huddles in a small alcove off of a narrow sub-hallway as crack smokers search the ship. Princess Sensimilla is a member of the Cannabis senate. The fear in her eyes gives way to anger as the muted sounds of approaching crack smokers grow louder, then one of the smokers spots her and radios to the others. "Set for stoned."

Sensimilla steps from her hiding place and blasts two smokers with her plasma pistol and starts to run but is felled by a psychedelic ray. The smokers rush up to inspect her inert body.

"She's stoned," one of them says. "She'll be alright. Report to Lord Raygun."

A short while later Princess Sensimilla is led down a low-ceilinged hallway by a squad of armored crack smokers. Her hands are bound and she is brutally shoved when she is unable to keep up with the briskly marching smokers. They stop in a smoke filled hallway as Ron Raygun emerges from the shadows and stops to stare hard at the frail young senator.

"Lord Raygun." The princess, who sounds like a valley girl, shakes her head. "I should have known. Only a dickhead like you could be so bold. The Inferior Senate will not sit still for this when they hear you've attacked a diplomatic…"

"Don't play stoner games with me your highness," Raygun hisses between breath tokes. "You weren't on any mercy mission. You passed through a restricted system. Several transmissions were beamed to this ship by spies who are now dead. What happened to the data they sent you?"

"I don't know what you are talking about. I'm a member of the Inferior Senate on a diplomatic mission to score some…"

"You're part of the Rasta Co-op and a traitor. Take her away!"

A crack smoker snaps to attention and raises his hand in the stiff nazi-like one finger salute. "Just say no!"

The princess is led down the hall into the smoldering hole blasted in the side of the ship.

An Inferior commander hurries to catch up to Raygun. "Holding her is dangerous! If word of this gets out it will generate sympathy for the rebellion. She should be smoked."

"My duty is to find those hidden grows of theirs. We have traced the rasta spies to her and now she is my only link to discovering their secret grows, and I intend to use it.

"She'll die before she gives you any dope."

"Leave that to me. Send a distress signal. Call it a meteorite storm, then inform her father and the senate that all aboard were smoked."

A cadre of crack smokers approach Raygun and the commander and snap to attention giving the salute.

"The data is not on board this ship," the leader reports. "No transmissions were made. A malfunctioning vapepod was jettisoned during the fighting, but we've confirmed that no life forms were aboard."

"They must have put the data in the vapepod cartridge. Send a detachment down to retrieve it but don't attract attention, then vaporize this ship and don't leave anything." Raygun turned to the commander. "That dope could be damaging. I want the stolen data destroyed at all costs. See to it personally, commander.

The commander puts his fist to his forehead with a middle finger salute and gave the Dank Lord a short bow. "Yes, your assholiness."

SIX

On the planet Tryptamine, Humboldt is considered No Man's Land where the rugged desert mesas meet the foreboding dune sea. In the midst of it the two helpless dopebots kick up clouds of shimmering rainbow dust as they leave the vapepod and work their way across the desert coastline.

MEO scans the horizon. "What a forsaken place this is. We seem to be made to suffer. I've got to rest before I fall apart. My joints are practically smoking."

Twocee makes a sharp right turn and starts off toward the rocky desert mesas. MEO stops and yells at him. "Where do you think you're going?"

A series of beeps, whistles, and bong hits pour forth from Twocee.

MEO waves a limp wrist. "Well, I'm not going that way. It's too rocky," he lisps. "This way is much easier. What makes you think there are any settlements *that* way?"

Twocee counters with beeps and a long gurgling bong hit.

"Don't get testicle with me. I've had just about enough of you. Go that way, go on! You'll be malfunctioning within a day you nearsighted scrap pile." He shoves Twocee and the tiny dopebot tumbles down a small dune. MEO starts off in the direction of the vast dune sea as little Twocee struggles to his treaded feet.

"And don't let me catch you following me begging for help because you won't get it!"

Twocee's reply is a rude sounding wet fart sound. He turns and rolls off in the direction of the towering mesas.

After parting ways with Twocee, MEO, hot with his shifting psychedelic plasma surface fading, struggles up over the ridge of a dune past the bleached bones of a toad-like beast, only to find more dunes that seem to go on endlessly. He looks back in the direction of the now distant rock mesas. "You malfunctioning roach clip. You tricked me into going this way but you'll do no better." He sits in a huff of anger, knocking shimmering sand from his joints. His plight appears hopeless when a glint of reflected rainbow light in the distance reveals an object moving toward him. MEO waves frantically and different colored grid patterns flash over his body at the approaching transport. "Hello! Over here! This way."

A few miles away swirling multicolored twin suns are setting beyond the edge of a narrow rock canyon where huge green glowing rock formations are shrouded in a foreboding psychedelic mist and the ominous sounds of otherworldly creatures. Twocee moves cautiously through the creepy rock canyon making tentative bong hit gurgles that imply fear and curiosity until he hears a hard metallic sound and stops.

A pebble tumbles down the canyon wall and a small dark figure darts into the shadows. A little further up the canyon a flicker of light reveals a pair of psychedelic spiraling eyes in the dark recesses a few feet from the narrow path.

The unsuspecting dopebot waddles along the rugged trail until a luminescent ray shoots out of the rocks engulfing him in an eerie glow. He manages one short electronic squeak and an electronic UH OH! sound and topples over onto his back. His facial display shows surprise, then flickers off, on, and off again.

Three furtive characters no taller than Twocee wearing grubby hemp cloaks with hoods that make them look like blunts with cone shaped bodies that end in fatter heads scurry out of the rocks. They holster weapons that look like Bic lighters and approach Twocee. Their faces are shrouded so that only their glowing orange spiraling eyes can be seen brightening and dimming with each inhale and exhale. They hiss and make odd guttural smoking and toking sounds and spew smoke as they heave Twocee onto their shoulders and carry him off.

In momentary bursts of video Twocee glimpses an imposing treaded trapezoidal fortress used by the blunts for transportation and shelter. The huge sand-pitted trimcrawler is equipped with a magnetic suction tube for sucking droids and scrap into their cargo chambers. Twocee's last flicker of vision is of the suction tube coming down and swallowing him into green-tinged blackness.

A short while later his power is restored with a small disk attached to his front when Twocee enters a wide room with a low ceiling. In its middle a dozen or so dopebots of various shapes and sizes are engaged in electronic conversation. Most are trimming cannabis buds while others carry off bins of finished buds. A voice of recognition calls out from the gloom.

"Twocee! It's you! It's you!" MEO scrambles up to Twocee and embraces him. He also has a small disk attached to his chest and his shifting body displays are muted.

SEVEN

Eight Inferior Senators and generals sit around a dark green conference table in the Death Bong conference room surrounded by walls of flickering displays. One full wall shows a panoramic view of star systems, galaxies, and other ships in their fleet moving parallel to them while smaller finned Inferior Thai Stick fighter escorts zip past resembling angry wasps. Six Inferior Crack Smokers stand guard around the room.

A young weaselly looking general, Commander Sessions stands at the end of the table. "This Spliff Lord sent by the Hempress Nancy will be our undoing. Until this Death Bong is fully operational we are vulnerable. The Rasta Co-op are more dangerous than you realize."

A short squat overweight Admiral Mota squirms in his chair. "Dangerous to your hempfleet commander, not to this Death Bong. Lord Raygun knows what he's doing. The rebellion will continue only as long as those cowards have a sanctuary."

All heads turn as Commander Sessions' speech is cut short by the entrance of the Grand Oxy Contin, Governor of the Inferior Outland Regions followed by the Dank Spliff Lord, Ron Raygun. All of the generals stand and put their fists to their foreheads with a middle finger salute and bow before the evil looking Governor as he takes his place at the head of the table. The Dank Lord stands behind him.

"I just received word that the Hempress has dissolved the Council," Oxy Contin bellows, "and the last remnants of the old weed republic have been swept away."

Commander Sessions drops down into his chair. "What about the rebellion? If the rebels have obtained a testicle readout of this Death Bong they might find a weakness and exploit it."

"The testicle data you're referring to will soon be back in our hands," Raygun says after a long toke sounding inhale.

Mota makes a dismissive gesture. "Any attack against this bong by the Rasta Co-op would be a useless gesture no matter what testicle data they have. Our bong is the ultimate power in the universe."

Raygun makes a masturbating motion with his fist and a smoking joint floats into his hand. He takes a long thoughtful hit before speaking. "Don't be too proud of this technological terror you created. The ability to destroy a planet or whole system is insignificant next to the Cosmic Buzz."

Mota snorts. "Don't try to frighten us with your psychonaut's ways, Lord Raygun. Your sad devotion to that ancient religion has not helped you conjure those stolen vape cartridges or given you clairvoyance enough to find the rebel's hidden grows."

Raygun takes a long hit off the joint and stares at Mota who chokes and starts to turn bright green under Raygun's spell.

Raygun blows smoke out from his mouthpiece and ears. "I find your lack of faith disturbing."

"Enough of this Raygun!" Contin demands. "Release him. This bickering is pointless. Lord Raygun will provide us with the location of the Rasta grow by the time this bong is operational. We will then crush this rebellion with one deep bong hit."

Raygun takes another toke. "As the Hempress Nancy wills it, so shall it be.

EIGHT

The trembling and bouncing of the trimcrawler stops, creating a commotion among the mechanical trimmers. MEO shakes Twocee and his dimmed display lights pop on displaying wide blinking eyes.

"Wake up! Wake up! We've stopped! We're doomed! Do you think they'll melt us down into pipe screens?"

A hatch opens filling the chamber with blinding white light and shimmering mist at the far end of the long chamber. A dozen or so blunts make their way through the odd assortment of trimming dopebots. Twocee and MEO are chosen and herded outside with several other unfortunates.

Five battered dopebots, including Twocee and MEO are lined up in front of the enormous trimcrawler that is parked beside a small homestead consisting of three large grow structures surrounded by several tall moisture vaporators and a small adobe block house all painted with faded paisley patterns. The blunts scurry around fussing over the dopebots, straightening them up or brushing dust from dented surfaces.

Blaze Bowlsmoker, a large burly dreadlocked man in his mid-fifties limps out of the shadows of a dingy side building smoking a long stemmed glass pipe followed by his slump-shouldered nephew, Dude Dopetoker.

One of the blunts walks ahead spouting an animated sales pitch in an unintelligible language as Dude and Blaze inspect the dopebots. A voice calls out from one of the grow structures and Dude goes over to find his Aunt Mary Jane standing in the courtyard.

"Dude, tell Blaze that if he gets a translator to be sure it speaks Rastafarian."

Blaze picks out a small hookah dopebot similar to Twocee and it waddles along behind him, then Blaze stops in front of MEO and studies him carefully. "Do you function in etiquette and protocol?"

MEO's skin brightens in a flurry of rainbow colored waves. "Protocol is my primary function. I am well versed in the customs and…"

"I don't need a protocol droid."

"Not in an environment like this, but I've been programmed for over thirty secondary functions that…"

"I need a droid that knows something about the binary language of moisture vaporators."

"My first job was programming binary load lifters. Very similar in most respects to your vaporators."

"Do you speak Rastafarian?"

"It's like a second language for me. I'm as fluent in Rastafarian…

"Shut up!"

"Shutting up, sir."

Blaze turns to the blunt beside him and jerks his thumb toward MEO. "I'll take this one," then he beckoned to Dude saying, "Take them to the garage. I want them cleaned up by dinner."

Disappointment shows on Dude's face. "But I was going into Hybrid Station to pick up some grow lights."

Blaze waves him off. "You can waste time with your friends after you finish your chores. Now get to it."

When the blunts move to lead the three remaining dopebots back into the trimcrawler, Twocee lets out a pathetic little beep and bong gurgle and starts after MEO, but is restrained by a blunt who zaps him with a control box while Blaze negotiates with the head blunt. Dude and the two dopebots start for the garage when a plate pops off the head of the 2-C unit spewing smoke and throwing pipes, roach clips, nuts, bolts, screws, springs, and other paraphernalia all over the ground.

"Uncle Blaze, this 2-C unit has a bad motivator. Look!" Dude adjusts the 2-C unit's head plate and it sparks and smokes wildly.

Blaze stares down the head blunt. "What kind of shit are you trying to push on us?"

The blunt goes into a loud spiel while Twocee moves back and forth flashing blue lights and making cop car siren sounds to attract attention. MEO taps Dude on the shoulder.

"If I might say so, sir, that 2-C unit is in top condition. A real bargain."

Dude points at Twocee. "Uncle Blaze! What about that one?"

Blaze argues with the blunt and the scruffy dwarf reluctantly trades the damaged hookah dopebot for 2CB. Blaze pays off the whining blunt as Dude and the two dopebots trudge off toward a grimy homestead entry.

MEO walks beside Twocee with an effeminate wave of his hand and leans down toward the little dopebot saying, "Why I stick my neck out for you is beyond my capacity."

The two dopebots follow Dude into a cluttered run down garage filled with the sweet scent of terpenes where MEO lowers himself into a large tub filled with warm hash oil in the center of the room. Dude puts little Twocee on top of a large battery beside Dude's battered weedspeeder and attaches a cord to his third eye.

"Thank the maker!" MEO says while wave after wave of luminescent colors pass over his skin. "This feels sooo good. I've got a bad case of dust contamination."

Twocee beeps a muffled reply. Dude looks lost in thought as he runs his hand over the damaged fin of a small two-man weedspeeder resting in a low hangar off the garage.

Dude sighs. "I'll never get out of here."

"I beg your pardon sir, but is there anything I might do to help?"

Dude glances at the dopebot and takes a long hit from a joint. "Not unless you can alter time, speed up the harvest, or teleport me off this rock."

"I'm only a droid and not very knowledgeable about such things. Not on this planet anyway. As a matter of fact, sir, I'm not even sure which planet I'm on."

"If there's a bright center to this universe, you're on the planet that's the furthest from it."

"I see, sir."

"Call me Dude."

"Yes Sir Duuuuuuude, MEO said, sounding like a surfer. "I am 5MEODMT, Human Cyborg relations and this is my counterpart 2CB. Dude unplugs Twocee and scrapes several connectors on the dopebot's head with a chrome pick and pipe cleaners. MEO climbs out of the hash oil tub and wipes oil from his shining reinvigorated colorful shifting patterned psychedelic body.

Dude pokes in deeper with his chrome pick. "There's a lot of resin buildup in his bowl. It looks like you both have seen a lot of weed."

"Indeed, Dude, sometimes I'm amazed we're in as good shape as we are with the rebellion and all."

Dude looks up from his work, sparked to life at the mention of rebellion. "You know about the rebellion?"

"That's how we came into your service."

"Were you in many battles?"

"Several. There is not much to tell. I'm nothing more than an interpreter and not very good at telling stories."

Dude struggles to remove a gooey fragment from Twocee's neck joint with a large pipe cleaner. "Well, my little friend, you've got something jammed in here real good. Were you a bud-trimmer or a..."

The fragment breaks loose with a snap, sending Dude tumbling. He sits up and sees a small 3-D hologram of Sensimilla projected from the third eye of little Twocee. The image is a rainbow of holographic colors that flicker in the dimly lit garage.

The beautiful Sensimilla hovers before them, her hands pressed together in prayer. "Doobie-wan Kenoobie. Smoke me! You're my only dope."

Dude's eyes grow wide. "What's this?"

Twocee's head rotates and looks around before beeping an answer for MEO to translate.

"Doobie-wan Kenoobie. Smoke me! You're my only dope," Sensimilla continues over and over again.

MEO turns different shades of pink and points at Sensimilla. "What is that?"

Twocee beeps his surprise and pretends he has just now become aware of the hologram and whistles and bong gurgles his reply.

"He says it's a malfunction," MEO says. "Old data, pay it no mind."

Dude is smitten and can't take his eyes off of Sensimilla. "Who is she? She's beautiful!"

"I think she was a passenger on our last voyage. A person of some importance I believe. Our captain was attached to..."

"Is there any more to this recording?"

Dude reaches for Twocee who lets out several frantic squeaks, a bong gurgle, and a middle finger display, then whistles and beeps a long message, punctuated by bong gurgles.

MEO shakes his head. "He says he is the property of Doobie-wan-Kenoobie, a resident of these parts, and it is a private message for him. Quite frankly sir, I don't know what he's talking about. Our last master was Captain Cannabinoid, but with all we've been through, I'm afraid poor little Twocee has become a bit eccentric."

"Doobie-wan-Kenoobie? I wonder if he means old Bud Kenoobie."

"Do you know him?"

"I don't know anyone named Doobie-wan, but old Bud lives out beyond the dune sea. Uncle Blaze says he's a sorcerer. He comes around here once in awhile to trade things, but I've hardly ever talked to him."

Dude's gaze goes back to the beautiful Sensimilla. "She must be important and it sounds to me like she's in trouble. Maybe the message is important. I should hear the rest of it." Dude reaches for Twocee and little Twocee squeaks faster, gurgles a blue streak, and flashes the finger again.

MEO nods slowly. "He says the restraining bolt has short circuited his recording system, but if you remove the restraining bolt he might be able to repeat the entire message."

Dude looks longingly at the princess and hasn't really heard what MEO said. "What? Oh yeah. I guess you're too small to run away if I take it off. I wonder what she's sending a message to old Bud for?" Dude takes a wedged bar, pops the retraining bolt off Twocee's side and the princess disappears. "Where did she go? Make her come back. Play back the whole message."

Twocee gurgles and flashes question marks.

"What message?" MEO asks, sounding annoyed. "The one you're carrying inside your resin clogged innards! I'm sorry sir, but he appears to have picked up a…"

"Dude! Dude, come to dinner," Mary Jane calls from another room.

Dude stands and shakes his head at the malfunctioning dopebot. "Coming Aunt Mary Jane!", then to MEO, "See what you can do with him. I'll be right back."

Dude tosses Twocee's restraining bolt on the work bench and hurries out of the room.

"You better consider playing that recording for him," MEO says.

Twocee farts.

NINE

Dude sits with Uncle Blaze at a table covered with steaming bowls of food. Aunt Mary Jane, a middle-aged woman with graying red hair and green eyes accented with crow's feet defined by deep laugh lines sets a pitcher of hemp milk down on the table and joins them.

Dude starts heaping food onto his plate. "I think that Twocee unit might have been stolen."

"What makes you think that?" Uncle Blaze asks as he pours everyone a glass of hemp milk from the pitcher.

"I stumbled on a recording while I was cleaning him. That droid claims to be the property of someone called Doobie-wan-Kenoobie."

Blaze's eyes grow wide at the mention of this name.

"I thought he might have meant old Bud," Dude continues. "The name is similar. Do you know what he's talking about?"

Uncle Blaze shakes his head. "It's a name from another time that can only mean trouble."

"Is he connected to old Bud? I didn't think he…"

"You stay away from that old stoner!" Uncle Blaze shakes his finger at Dude. "Do you hear me? He's a crazy old man!" Blaze turns red and continues shaking his finger. "He's dangerous and best left alone. That droid has nothing to do with him. Tomorrow I want you to take it to Flowerhead and have its memory flushed. I don't care where it came from. It belongs to us now."

"But what if this Doobie-wan comes looking for it?"

Blaze let out a long sigh. "I don't think he exists anymore. He died at the same time as your father. Now forget about it."

"Did he know my father?"

"I said forget about it!" Uncle Blaze says with a raised voice. "Your only concern is getting the new droids ready for tomorrow. The last of our savings are tied up in those two. In the morning I want you to have them working with the hydroponic units on the South ridge."

"Yes sir. I think these droids are going to work out fine. In fact I was thinking about our agreement about me staying on another season. If those new droids work out I want to transmit my application to the academy this year."

Blaze scowls and shakes his head. "You mean next term before the harvest?"

"You have more than enough droids."

"Droids can't replace you Dude, you know that. The harvest is when I need you the most. It's just one more season."

Dude toys with his food, not looking at his uncle.

"For the first time we have a fortune in dank bud coming into our hands," Uncle Blaze says in a placating voice. "We'll make enough this harvest to hire some extra hands, then you can go to the academy, but I need you here for now Dude."

Dude pushes his half-eaten plate of food aside and stands.

Aunt Mary Jane looks up at him, "Where are you going?"

"I have to finish cleaning those droids." Dude slouches out of the room while Uncle Blaze mechanically finishes his dinner.

Mary Jane rests her hand on his arm. "Blaze, we can't keep him here forever. Most of his friends are gone. It means so much to him."

"I'll make it up to him. I promise."

Dude's just not a grower, Blaze. He's got too much of his father in him."

"That's what I'm afraid of."

Dude stops on his way to the garage workshop to watch the giant twin psychedelic suns of Tryptamine slowly disappear behind a distant dune range before entering the domed entrance to the workshop. The dopebots are nowhere in sight when he steps inside. He takes a small control box from his utility belt similar to what the blunts carry and activates it, creating a low hum. MEO pops up from behind the speeder letting out a short yell.

"What are you hiding back there for?"

MEO stumbles forward, but Twocee is nowhere in sight.

"It wasn't my fault sir. Please don't deactivate me. I told him not to go but he's malfunctioning and kept babbling about his mission."

"Shit!" Dude races out of the garage followed by MEO out through the small domed entry to the homestead and searches the darkening horizon for Twocee. MEO struggles out behind him as

Dude scans the landscape with his binoculars. "He's nowhere in sight. Uncle Blaze is going to kill me."

"Begging your pardon, sir, but can't we go after him?"

"Not at night. It's too dangerous with all the weedpeople around. We'll have to wait until morning."

"Dude are you finished with those droids yet?" Blaze yells from the homestead plaza. "I'm turning the power down for the night."

"I'll be there in a few minutes." He turns and takes one final look across the dim horizon.

Early the following morning while Aunt Mary Jane prepares breakfast in the warm glow of the kitchen, Uncle Blaze storms in in a huff. "Have you seen Dude this morning?"

Aunt Mary Jane takes a pan of warm bread from the oven. "He said he had some things to do before he started today."

"Did he take the new droids with him?"

"I think so."

"He'd better have those hydroponic units on the South ridge repaired by midday or there'll be hell to pay."

TEN

Somewhere on the far edge of the dune sea a group of Inferior Crack Smokers mill about in front of the half buried vape pod that brought Twocee and MEO to Tryptamine.

"This is the one but there are no vape cartridges here, sir," one of the crack smokers yells to an officer some distance away.

A second smoker, standing next to the officer picks a small hash pipe out of the sand and gives it to the officer who examines it closely. "Droids!"

In another part of the desert MEO pilots Dude's sleek weedspeeder across the vast desert wasteland. The rock and sand of the desert floor are a shimmering rainbow colored blur as the flying speeder leaves a dense smoke trail in its wake while dude scans their surroundings with his electrobinoculars.

"Old Bud Kenoobie lives out in this direction somewhere, but I don't see how that Twocee unit could have come this far. We must have missed him. Wait! There's something on the scanner. It looks like our droid. Hit the accelerator!"

They close in on a rocky area on the coast line of the dune sea and cruise to a stop. Two weedpeople shrouded in grimy hemp cloaks peer over the edge of a rock mesa. One of them raises a long plasma rifle and points it at the speeder but the second creature grabs it before it can be fired.

After a short heated discussion they creep down the side of the mesa into a massive rock mesa canyon and scurry to two large Bufo toads tied to a rock. The monstrous toads are as large as elephants with huge multicolored spiraling psychedelic eyes. The raiders mount saddles strapped to the huge creatures and hop down the rugged bluff close to where the speeder is parked.

Dude stands bent over little Twocee with his plasma rifle slung over his shoulder. "Where do you think you're going?"

The little droid whistles and gurgles a feeble reply as MEO poses menacingly behind the little runaway.

"Master Dude here is your rightful owner," he admonishes. "We'll have no more of this Doobie-wan Kenoobie gibberish and don't talk to me about your mission. You're fortunate he doesn't blast you into a million pieces right here."

Dude looks around. "Come on. It's getting late. I hope we can get back before Uncle Blaze has a shit fit."

MEO stands up straight with his hands on his hips. "If you don't mind my saying so sir, I think you should deactivate the little fugitive until you've gotten him back to your workshop."

"He's not going to try anything."

The little dopebot jumps to life with a mass of frantic whistles, squeals, and bong gurgles.

Dude frowns. "What's wrong with him now?"

MEO's skin flashes fire engine red. "He says there are several creatures approaching from the Southeast."

Dude swings his rifle into position and looks to the South, but doesn't see anything so he makes his way to the top of a rock ridge and scans the canyon with his electrobinoculars. MEO struggles up behind him and spots the two riderless Bufo toads. "There are two Bufos down there but I don't see any – wait a second, they're weedpeople all right!"

Dude scans the horizon again and sees a distant raider through his electrobinoculars, then something moves in front of his field of view. Before Dude or MEO can react, a gruesome raider looms over them. MEO is startled and tumbles off the side of a cliff clanging, banging, and rattling down the side of a mountain.

The towering creature brings down a curved, double pointed axe blade, but Dude deflects the blow with his rifle which is smashed to pieces. He scrambles backward and is forced to the edge of a deep crevice. The raider stands over him with his weapon raised and lets out a shriek.

Twocee slips into the shadows of a small alcove in the rocks and remains motionless as the weedpeople walk past carrying the inert Dude who they drop beside the speeder, then they ransack the speeder, throwing parts and supplies in all directions until a great howling moan echoes throughout the canyon sending them fleeing.

Twocee moves tighter into the shadows as the howling moan grows closer until a shabby old desert rat of a man appears and leans over Dude. His ancient leathery face is set off by dark, penetrating eyes and a scraggly white beard. He squints as he scrutinizes the unconscious farm boy, then Twocee makes a sound and the man turns and looks right at him. "Hello there! Come here my little friend. Don't be afraid."

Twocee waddles over to where Dude lies in a heap and whistles, beeps, and gurgles his concern. The old man puts his hand on Dude's forehead, lights a pipe, and blows smoke into Dude's face shotgun style using the barrel of the broken plasma rifle and Dude comes to blinking wildly.

"Don't worry, he'll be all right," the old man says to the two dopebots.

Dude looks up wide-eyed. "What happened?"

"Rest easy, son. You're fortunate you're still in one piece."

"Bud? Bud Kenoobie am I glad to see you!"

"The Shakeland wastes are not to be traveled lightly. Tell me young Dude, what brings you out this far?"

"This little droid is searching for his former master. I've never seen such devotion in a droid before. There seems to be no stopping him. He claims to be the property of someone called Doobie-wan Kenoobie. Is he a relative of yours?"

Bud ponders this, scratching his scruffy beard. "Doobie-wan Kenoobie. Doobie-wan. Now that's a name I haven't heard in a long time. Most curious…"

"My Uncle Blaze said he was dead."

"Oh, he's not dead. Not yet."

"You know him!"

"I haven't gone by the name of Doobie-wan since before you were born."

"Then this droid does belong to you."

"Can't seem to remember ever owning a droid. Most interesting." He glances up at the overhanging cliffs. "It's best we get inside. The weedpeople are easily startled but they will return in greater numbers."

Dude sits up and rubs his head. Twocee lets out a pathetic beep causing Dude to look around. "MEO!"

Little Twocee rolls over to the edge of a large sand pit chattering away in whistles, beeps, and gurgles. Dude and Bud follow him and find a dented, tangled MEO lying half buried in the sand with one of his arms broken off. Dude tries to revive the inert dopebot by shaking him and flips a switch on his back several times until MEO's systems turn on in flashing geometric patterns that move across his body. His eyes move in shifting polychromatic geometries "Where am I? Oh, I'm sorry, sir. I must have taken a bad step…"

"Can you stand? We have to get out of here before the raiders come back."

Dude and Bud help the battered dopebot to his feet while Twocee watches from the top of the pit. Bud glances around sensing something and stands up to sniff the air. "Quickly son, they're on the move."

ELEVEN

Following directions from Bud, Dude pilots the weedspeeder through a maze of narrow canyons until they come to the hidden entrance to a secluded cave. The small spartan hovel is cluttered with paraphernalia, but radiates an air of comfort and security. Dude sits in an old chair beside MEO and focuses on repairing MEO's arm while Bud fiddles with Twocee. "Now let's see if we can't figure out what you are my little friend and where you came from."

Dude looks up. "I saw part of a message he…"

Twocee's third eye flickers to life and a burst of polychromatic laser confetti flies into the air followed by the holographic video of the beautiful Sensimilla that fills the space in front of him.

Bud nods. "I seem to have found it."

Dude stops his work and stares at the lovely Sensimilla's image while she speaks.

"General Doobie-Wan Kenoobie, I present myself in the name of the royal family of Cannabis and the Co-op to restore the Grow Republic. I break your solitude at the bidding of my father Purple Diesel, Viceroy and Chairman of the Cannabis system. Years ago you served the Republic in the Clone Wars. Now he begs you to aid us again in our most desperate hour. He is asking you to join him on our home planet Cannabis. I regret that I am unable to present my father's request to you in person. My mission to return with you has failed. Information vital to the survival of the Co-op has been placed in this droid's vape cartridge. My father will know how to retrieve it. I plead with you to see this 2-C unit safely delivered to Cannabis. Please help me Doobie-wan. You are my only dope."

Static fills the air and the transmission is cut short. Bud leans back, scratches his head, and puffs on a tarnished chrome pipe.

Dude has stars in his eyes and lets out a long sigh. "She is smoking hot! You fought in the Clone Wars?"

"I was once a Red Eye Knight like your father."

"Red Eye Knight? My father didn't fight in the wars. He was a navigator on a DMT freighter."

"So your Uncle Blaze told you. He didn't agree with your father's ideals and thought he should have stayed here and not gotten involved. He was afraid your father's adventures might influence you."

Dude hangs his head. "I wish I'd known him."

"He was the best vapefighter pilot in the galaxy, a clever warrior, and a good friend. I understand you've become quite a good pilot yourself. In many ways you're much like your father." Bud gets up and goes to a battered chest where he rummages around. "Which reminds me, I have something here that your father wanted you to have, but your uncle wouldn't allow it. He believed you might follow old Doobie-wan on some idealistic crusade like your father did."

Dude finishes repairing MEO and starts to put the restraining bolt back on, then thinks about it for a moment and puts it on the table. Bud sits down across from Dude and hands him a short handle that looks like a small blowtorch with several electronic devices attached to it. A vial of white powder hangs from its end on a thick gold chain wrist strap. Dude puts the chain on his wrist. "What's this?"

"Your father's pipe blazer and some powdered Bufo venom. At one time these were widely used and they still are in some parts of the galaxy."

Dude pushes a button on the handle and a long psychedelic plasma shoots out about four feet and flickers there.

"This is the weapon of a Red Eye Knight," Bud says with conviction, "which is not as a clumsy or random as a blaster. It's an elegant weapon. For over a thousand generations Red Eye Knights were the most powerful, most respected Buzz in the galaxy. That was when the galactic senate ruled the galaxy before the dark times, before the Hempire."

"How did my father die?"

"He was betrayed and murdered by a young Red Eye, Ron Raygun, a boy I was training. One of my brightest disciples and one of my greatest failures. He used the power of the Buzz for evil to help the Hempire hunt down and destroy the Red Eye Knights. Now the Red Eye are all but extinct. Raygun was seduced by Hempress Nancy and the dank side of the Buzz and they consumed him.

"The Buzz?"

"The Buzz is something a Red Eye deals with. It surrounds us, binds the galaxy together, and directs our actions. Knowledge of the Buzz is what gives a Red Eye his power. You must learn the ways of the Buzz if you are to come with me to Cannabis."

"Cannabis? I can't go to Cannabis. I've got to get back home! It's late and I'm in for it as it is. Uncle Blaze is going to kick my ass! You can take the droid. I'll think of something to tell my uncle. I hope…"

"I need your help, Dude. I'm getting old for this sort of thing."

"I can't get involved I have work to do. I don't like the Hempire. I hate it, but there is nothing I can do about it right now."

"That's your uncle talking."

"My uncle. How am I going to explain all this?"

Remember, the Buzz is with all men and binds them together. The suffering of one is the suffering of all."

"I can take you as far as Bongwater. You can get transport there to the Shulgin spaceport at Mendocino or wherever you're going."

"You must follow your bliss, Bro, if that is what you feel."

"Right now I don't feel too good."

TWELVE

Two crack smokers open an electronic cell door in a prison cell corridor deep within the bowels of the Death Bong and allow several Inferior guards to enter. Princess Sensimilla's face is filled with defiance which gives way to fear as a giant forest green multitentacled torture dopebot enters, followed by Ron Raygun.

"Now your *highness*, we will discuss the location of the hidden rasta grow," Raygun says between toking sounds. The door slides shut and the muffled cries of the rasta princess are barely heard.

Down on Tryptamine Dude's speeder stops before the smoking remains of the huge blunt trimcrawler. Dude and Bud walk around studying the smoldering rubble and scattered bodies.

"Looks like the weedpeople did it alright." Dude points at some markings in the sand. "There's Bufo tracks." He shakes his head. "We've never heard of them hitting something this big."

Bud crouches down in the sand and studies the tracks. "They didn't, but we were meant to think so. Whoever left here rode side by side. Weedpeople always ride in single file to hide their numbers. Look at these blast points. Weedpeople are not this accurate. Only Inferior crack smokers are this precise.

"These were the same blunts who sold us Twocee and MEO. Why would Inferior smokers be smoking blunts?" Dude looks back at the speeder and sees Twocee and MEO doing their own inspection of the smoking blunts. "If they tracked the dopebots to the blunts they may have learned who they sold them to which would lead them back…"

Dude races for the speeder and jumps in.

"Wait Dude," Ben calls out. "It's too dangerous."

Dude races off across the bleak salt flats leaving Bud and the two dopebots alone with the smoldering trimcrawler and his worst fears are realized when he sees dark green smoke in the distance. He skirts a couple of small bluffs before the speeder roars up to Uncle Blaze and Aunt Mary Jane's burning homestead. Dude jumps out and runs to the smoking craters that were once his home. Debris and paraphernalia are scattered everywhere. "Aunt Mary Jane! Uncle Blaze!"

Dude stumbles around in a frenzy looking for his aunt and uncle until he finds his uncle's broken long stemmed glass pipe amidst their smoldering remains.

High above in an orbit around Tryptamine Ron Raygun and the regional Governor Oxy Contin stand before the huge screen in the Death Bong control room. Short, stocky Admiral Mota waddles up to them smoking a twisted elaborate multicolored LED vape pen with his pinkie finger extended as if drinking from a fancy tea cup.

"The final check out is complete and all systems are operational. What course shall we set?"

Raygun makes a long toking sound followed by a little cough. "The princess has a great deal of control. Her resistance to the rectal probe is considerable. It will be sometime before we can extract any useful information from her. I think it is time we demonstrated the full power of this Death Bong. Set your course for Cannabis."

A psychedelic flash fills the sky above the decimated trimcrawler where a large bonfire of smoldering dead Blunts burns with rainbow colored flames as Bud and the dopebots look on.

Dude pulls up in the speeder sobbing with his head hung low.

"There is nothing you could have done, Dude." Bud pulls out a vial and a small iridescent tube from his robes. "Had you been there, you'd now be dead and the droids would be in the hands of the Hempire." He empties a small glittering pile of powder from his vial and takes a snort with the tube before offering it to Dude who follows suit. "The Buzz is with you."

Dude takes a snort and brightens a little. "That's good shit! I'll take you to the spaceport at Mendocino. I want to go with you to Cannabis. There's nothing here for me now. I want to learn the ways of the Buzz and become a Red Eye like my father."

THIRTEEN

The speeder stops on a bluff overlooking the Shulgin spaceport at Mendocino where ships resembling pipes, bongs, vaping pens, and other smoking devices of differing shapes and sizes take off and land from all directions like hummingbirds darting to and from to a feeder. A haphazard array of low psychedelically painted structures and domes line its streets. A harsh breeze blows shimmering fluorescent sand across the stark canyon floor as dusk approaches. Dude adjusts his goggles with spinning lenses and walks to the edge of the craggy bluff where Bud is standing.

Bud takes a quick snort from his palm with his glittering tube. "There it is. Shulgin Spaceport. You won't find a more wretched hive of scum, roaches, and fuckery. The Hempire is on the alert so we have to be very cautious."

Dude scowls and looks up giving Bud a determined smile. "I'm ready for anything."

Bud holds out his palm and offers Dude a snort from the tube. "This will help you keep your edge."

Dude leans down and takes a huge snort and pops up wide-eyed making a series of rapid snoring sounds, followed by a goofy smile, then they jump into the speeder and fly at top speed toward the spaceport, slowing when they reach the city's limits before coming to a stop behind a line of assorted speeder vehicles on a crowded street near its center. When they get to the front of the line several combat hardened crack smokers surround them looking over the two dopebots. Their leader sidles up to Dude. "How long have you had these droids?"

"Three or four harvests."

"They're up for sale if you want them," Bud adds.

The crack smoker waves him off. "Did you come from the South?"

"Ahh… No. We live in the West near Bongwater."

The crack smoker crosses his arms. "Let me see your Medical Marijuana Identification cards."

When Dude fumbles for his I.D. Bud speaks to the smoker in a controlled monotone.

"You don't need to see his identification."

The crack smoker uncrosses his arms. "I don't need to see your identification."

Bud follows up with, "These aren't the dopebots you're looking for."

The crack smoker looks to his men. "These aren't the dopebots we're looking for."

Bud finishes with, "He can go on about his business."

"You can go on about your business."

Bud nods. "Just say no. Move along now."

The crack smoker waves them forward. "Just say no. Move along now."

The speeder pulls up to a rundown cantina on the outskirts of the spaceport. A huge pulsating marquee hangs over the entrance that says **LEARY'S LOUNGE** with smaller flashing suggestive signs surrounding the main one in day-glo colors. The most prominent one of them says **TURN ON, TUNE IN, AND DROP OUT!** Various transports resembling smoking paraphernalia, including several unusual beasts of burden are parked outside. A blunt runs up and fondles the speeder. Dude shoos it away.

"I can't abide those overstuffed blunts," MEO says. "Disgusting creatures!"

Dude shakes his head. "I can't understand how we got by those crack smokers."

"The Buzz is a strong influence on the mind," Bud says. "It's a powerful ally, but as you come to know it, you will discover that it can also be a danger."

"Do you really think we can find a pilot who will take us to Cannabis?"

"Most of the good freighter pilots frequent bars here but watch your step, this place can get a little trippy."

Dude and his two mechanical servants follow Bud into the smoke-filled cantina where muted variegated lasers and flashing lights shoot through the smoke. The murky den is filled with weird and exotic

DMT creatures, machine elves, and monsters at a long metallic bar. Twocee rotates his head, taking it all in while playing an electronic version of the opening of THE GOOD, THE BAD, AND THE UGLY theme.

One-eyed, thousand-eyed, multiple bizarre-nosed alien creatures are everywhere. Slimy, leafy, scaly tentacles and claws huddle over glowing drinks, hookahs, pipes, and other smoking paraphernalia while others snort long lines of different colored fluorescent powders. Bud and Dude move to an empty spot at the bar near a group of repulsive human Columbian pirates. A huge rough-looking Budtender floats over to Dude.

"Your dopebots will have to wait outside. We don't serve 'em here."

Dude looks to old Bud who is talking to one of the Columbian pirates and notices several of the gruesome creatures at the bar glaring at him.

"Yes, of course. I'm sorry."

Dude turns to MEO. "You'd better stay with the speeder. We don't want any shit from anybody in here."

MEO looks around and nods rapidly. "I heartily agree with you sir."

MEO and Twocee go outside and most of the creatures at the bar go back to smoking, drinking, and snorting. Bud is standing next to an eight foot tall savage-looking creature resembling a huge green cola bud with fierce baboon-like fangs. His large sparkling emerald green eyes dominate a leaf covered face that looks like a smaller cannabis cola version of his body. He wears two bandoliers of vape cartridges over his leafy body, a flak jacket painted in a cannabis leaf pattern, and green hemp cloth shorts.

Bud speaks to the huge doobie, pointing to Dude several times during his conversation and the huge creature lets out a horrifying laugh that sounds more like a high-pitched growl. Dude is disconcerted and pretends not to hear the conversation between Bud and the giant doobie but tries not to show it. He quietly smokes from a one-hitter, looking over the crowd for a sympathetic ear. A large multiple-eyed cannabis bud looking creature gives Dude a rough shove, snarling, "Smokety roach dopety!"

The hideous freak is obviously very stoned. Dude tries to ignore It and turns away, but a short, grubby humanoid and an even smaller roach headed beast join the belligerent monstrosity and the big creature yells unintelligible gibberish at Dude.

"Don't insult us," the humanoid says in a gravelly voice. "You just watch yourself. We're wanted men. I have the death sentence on twelve systems."

The roach lets out a loud gurgling grunt and everything at the bar moves away. Dude tries to remain cool but his three adversaries ready their weapons and Bud moves in behind Dude.

"This little roach isn't worth the effort. Come, let me buy you some edibles..."

A powerful blow from the unpleasant multiple-eyed creature sends Dude crashing through tables and breaking a large water pipe filled with foul looking vomit colored bong water. The monster draws a chrome plasma pistol from his belt with a blood curdling shriek and levels it at old Bud.

"No blasters! No blasters!" the budtender says in a panic.

With astounding agility, Bud's pipe blazer sparks to life and in a flash a smoking arm lies on the floor. The roach is cut in two and the giant, multiple-eyed creature lies doubled over, cut from chin to groin. Bud turns off his pipe lighter and replaces it on his belt. Dude, shaking and amazed at the old man's abilities, struggles to stand. The entire fight only lasted seconds. The cantina goes back to normal, although Bud is given a respectable amount of room at the bar. Dude, rubbing his head, approaches him with new awe.

Bud gestures toward the eight foot tall savage-looking cannabis bud creature with the fierce fangs. "This is O.G. Chronic, first mate on a ship that might suit our needs."

FOURTEEN

Dude is giddy and takes another toke from his one-hitter as he follows Bud and O.G. to a booth where Hash Stoner, a tough James Dean type vapepilot about thirty years old is sitting. A sexy perfectly shaped MDMA Love Droid has her arms around him.

He sends her bouncing on her way with a pat on the ass as the group approaches. "Beat it Ecstasy!"

Hash looks up at Bud who slides into the seat across from him followed by Dude. "You're pretty handy with that blazer old man. Not often one sees that kind of blazer play on this side of the galaxy. I'm Hash Smoker, Captain of the Pineapple Express. OhGee tells me you're looking for passage to Cannabis."

"Yes indeed. If it's a fast ship."

With an exaggerated expression of surprise, Hash says, "You've never heard of the Pineapple Express?"

"Should I?"

"It's the ship that made the Ketamine run in less than a dozen bong hits! I've outrun Inferior starships, not the local stash cruisers mind you. These are the big Columbian ships I'm talking about. I think she's fast enough for you old man. What's your cargo?"

"Myself, the boy, and two droids, with no questions asked."

"No questions. Local trouble?"

"Let's just say we'd like to avoid any Inferior entanglements."

"These days that can be a real trick. It will cost you about ten thousand shatterbucks in advance."

"Ten thousand!" Dude says coughing out smoke. "We could almost buy our own ship for that."

"But could you fly it?"

Dude starts to get up. "You bet I could! I'm not such a bad pilot myself. I don't…

Bud pulls Dude back down. "We don't have that much but we can pay you two thousand now and another fifteen when we reach Cannabis."

Hash thinks about it for a few moments then says, "That's seventeen. You've got yourselves a ship. Docking bay four twenty. We can take off as soon as you're ready." He inclines his head toward the bar. "Looks like someone's taking an interest in your handicraft."

Bud and Dude turn around to see four Inferior crack smokers looking at the dead bodies and asking the budtender questions. By the time the budtender points to the booth, Dude and Bud have slipped away. The crack smokers look back to the budtender who shrugs.

Outside the bar Dude and Bud secure Twocee to the back of the weedspeeder and take off in a puff of smoke.

"If the speed of Stoner's ship is as fast as his boasting," Bud says, "we should do well."

Dude shakes his head. "But it will be expensive."

"I'm afraid you'll have to sell your weedspeeder."

"It's all right. I'm never coming back to this shit hole planet."

Back inside the cantina the crack smokers who questioned the budtender walk past Hash and O.G. giving them both a careful check out. Hash turns to the giant doobie and says in a low voice, "OhGee, this charter could save our neck. Seventeen thousand! Those two really must be desperate."

As Hash and O.G. slide out of the booth, a slimy purple bud-faced alien with a short smoking trunk nose pokes a gun in Hash's side and speaks with an electronically translated staccato voice punctuated by puffs of smoke. "Going somewhere, Stoner?"

"As a matter of fact I was just going to see your boss. Tell Bubba I have his money."

"Then I'll take it now."

Hash sits back down and the alien sits across from him holding the gun on him. "I don't have it here with me. Tell Bubba…"

"It's too late. Bubba would rather have your ship."

"Over my dead body."

"That's the idea Stoner. You will come outside with me or should I finish it here?"

The slimy alien disappears in a blinding psychedelic plasma flash and a huge puff of sickly green colored smoke. Hash pulls his plasma gun from beneath the table as the other patrons look on in bemused amazement. Hash gets up and starts out of the cantina, flipping the budtender a bag of weed as he leaves. "Sorry for the mess."

Bud and Dude cruise down a cluttered alleyway off of a Mendocino side street to a sleazy used speeder lot with a lopsided sign that says **HOFMANN'S BICYCLE EMPORIUM**, where all the vehicles look like pipes, vapes, chillums, and one-hitters. A tall grotesque, mushroom-headed used speeder dealer emerges from a crowd of strange exotic creatures and spindly legged beasts. The mushroom creature concludes the sale by giving Dude some cannabis and vape cartridges while speaking in a strange unintelligible tongue.

"He says it's the best he can do." Dude shakes his head. "Since the LSD-25 came out, these models just aren't in demand."

Bud pats Dude on the back. "It will be sufficient. I've got enough to cover the rest."

Dude throws up his hands and together with MEO and Twocee in tow they walk to the main street leading to the Shulgin space port where Bubba the Kush, a disgusting drooling hulk of a mushroom sprouting blob stands in the middle of Docking Bay 420 with half a dozen grisly purple, green, blue, and gray alien pirates. His voice sounds like a wet fart with a southern accent when he speaks. "Come out Stoner!" he gurgles.

A voice from behind the pirates startles them and they turn around to see Hash Stoner and the giant doobie O. G. standing behind them with no weapons in sight.

"I've been waiting for you Bubba," Hash says.

"Hash, my boy," Bubba says in a fatherly smooth gurgle. "There are times when you disappoint me. Why haven't you paid me? And why did you have to smoke poor Roach like that?"

"You sent Roach to smoke me."

"Hash! Hash! If only you hadn't dumped that shipment of wax and shatter. You understand I can't make exceptions. Where would I be if every pilot who smuggled for me dumped their shipment at the first sign of an Inferior starship?"

"You know, even I get boarded sometimes, Bubba. I had no choice, but I've got a charter now and I can pay you back, plus a little extra. I just need more time."

Bubba gestures to his men with tyrannosaurus like arms. "Put your blasters away. Hash my boy, I'm only doing this because I need you, so for an extra twenty percent dab I'll give you a little more time, but this is it. If you disappoint me again, I'll put a price on your head so large you won't be able to go near a civilized system for the rest of your life."

FIFTEEN

O.G. Chronic waits at the entrance to Docking Bay 420 for Bud, Dude, and the dopebots jabbering and signaling for them to hurry when he sees them. O.G. looks around furtively before leading the group into the dirt pit that is Docking Bay 420. Resting in the middle of the huge hole is a large round battered water pipe looking craft.

Hash Stoner comes down the boarding ramp exhaling a big puff of smoke. "She may not look like much, but she's got it where it counts. I've added some special modifications myself. She'll make point four two zero beyond pipe speed."

Dude looks at the ship and shakes his head. O.G. rushes up the ramp ahead of them and urges the others to follow.

"We're a little rushed so if you'll hurry aboard we'll be off," Hash says as everyone rushes up the gang plank past a grinning Hash Stoner into the cockpit of the Pineapple Express. O.G. settles into the pilot's chair and starts the smoking engines of the starship which ramp up with the sound of a long toke from a joint and spews puffs that look and smell like cannabis exhales. Spiraling and flashing cannabis symbol themed displays and a series of slider controls that look like weed pipes and vape pens come to life with various inhaling and snorting sounds when they are activated.

Outside eight Inferior Crack Smokers rush up to the door of the docking bay with rifles that look like bongs at the ready and come charging down the docking bay entrance. Hash sees them rushing into the bay firing different colored smoking plasma rays at him as he ducks into the spaceship. "OhGee! Deflector screens quick! Get us out of here!"

Hash draws his plasma pistol and fires a couple of rainbow colored shots, forcing the crack smokers to dive for safety. The starship engines whine and Hash hits a release button that slams the entry ramp shut.

A group of crack smokers at a check point out on the street hear the general alarm and look to the sky as Pineapple Express rises above the dingy outpost and disappears into the morning sky while Hash climbs into the pilot's chair next to O.G. who chatters away and points to a pulsating spiral display making a whoop whoop sound.

Hash nods. "It looks like an Inferior Cruiser. Our passengers must be hotter than a crack pipe. Try to hold it off and angle the deflectors until I can make the calculations for the jump to pipe speed."

A few moments later the Pineapple Express races away from the psychedelic planet Tryptamine, followed by three huge Inferior star destroyers that look like glass and metal pipes and a bong.

Inside the Pineapple Express Dude and Bud make their way into the cramped cockpit where Hash continues his calculations. "Stay sharp OhGee, we've got two more coming in. They're going to try to cut us off."

Dude shakes his head. "I thought you said this thing was fast."

"Watch your mouth, kid," Hash snaps, "or you'll find yourself floating home. We'll be safe enough once we jump into hybridspace. They can't track us accurately at pipe speeds and I know a few maneuvers that should lose them."

The ship shudders as an explosion flashes outside the window.

"How long before you can make the jump to pipe speed?" Bud asks.

"It'll take a few minutes for the galactic positioning system to calculate the coordinates."

Dude snorts in disbelief. "At the rate they're gaining..."

Hash turns to him. "Traveling through hybridspace isn't like dusting crops, boy. Without calculations we could pass right through a star or bounce into a supernova."

The ship rocks violently as MEO clutches his seat back in the main hold area while Twocee sways to and fro under the impact of plasma blasts.

"I forgot how much I hate space travel," MEO mutters.

Dude and Bud enter and strap themselves into their chairs.

SIXTEEN

Admiral Mota enters the Death Bong control room and gives the middle finger salute while bowing before Governor Toking who stands before a wall screen displaying a small green, red, purple colored planet that resembles a cannabis bud. "We are entering the Trichrome star system. We await your orders."

Raygun enters with his robes fluttering like a giant bat followed by two crack smokers dragging Princess Sensimilla by each arm. She makes a disgusted gagging sound. "Governor Toking, I should've expected to find you holding that dick head Raygun's leash. I recognized your skunk weed stench when I was brought on board."

"Charming to the last," Mota says, sounding like he is speaking through a helium exhale. "You don't know how hard I found it signing the order to terminate your life."

"I'm surprised you had the balls to take responsibility yourself."

"Princess Sensimilla, before your execution I would like you to be my guest at a ceremony that will make this Death Bong operational. No star system will dare oppose the Hempress Nancy after we demonstrate the power of this Death Bong's paraquat ray. You have already had the honor of determining the choice of the planet that will be destroyed first. Since you are reluctant to provide us with the location of the rasta grow base I have chosen to test the bong's destructive power on your home planet of Cannabis."

"No! Cannabis is peaceful. We have no weapons. You can't…"

"You would prefer another target? A military target? Name the system! I grow tired of asking this, so it will be the last time. Where is the rasta underground grow?"

An intercom announces, "All stations code green. We are approaching Cannabis."

"Ketamine," Sensimilla says softly. "They're on Ketamine."

Toking looks to the Dank Spliff Lord and bows. "There, you see Raygun? She can be reasonable," then he turns to the others. "Proceed with the operation and fire when ready."

The princess gasps. "What?"

Toking shakes his head slowly. "Ketamine is too remote to be an effective demonstration. We will deal with our rasta friends soon enough."

The Death Bong shakes with an exceptionally loud gurgle and a stream of concentrated fluttering psychedelic smoke hits the small green, red, and purple bud colored planet. It glows orange and is blown into smoking space dust by the Paraquat ray and Princess Sensimilla seethes with rage. "And you call yourselves humans?"

"You are far too trusting. You will shortly see your hopeless rebellion vanish in a similar fashion."

Back in the main hold compartment of the Pineapple Express Bud falters and almost faints, then rubs his forehead as if he has a headache."

"What is it? Dude asks. "What's wrong?"

"I feel a great ebbing in the Buzz. The cry of a billion tokes stopping all at once. Something terrible has happened." Bud drifts into a momentary trance, then fixes his gaze on Dude. "Continue with your exercise."

Hash enters and begins checking various screen readouts. "You can stop worrying about your troubles with those Inferior crack heads. I told you I'd lose them."

Nobody says anything and Hash says, "Don't everybody thank me at once. Anyway, I calculate our arrival on Cannabis at four twenty."

Dude stands in the middle of the small hold area and seems frozen in place with a humming pipe blazer held high over his head. Bud watches him from the corner studying his movements while Hash watches with a smug look and O.G. looks on with interest.

"Remember Dude, a Red Eye warrior can feel the Buzz flowing from him."

"You mean it controls your actions?"

"It depends on how stoned you are, but it also obeys your commands."

Suspended at eye level about ten feet in front of Dude, a baseball sized cannabis bud covered with antenna that looks like sparkling kief hovers slowly in a wide arc. The bud floats to one side of Dude, then to the other before making a blazing lunge that stops inches from his face. Dude doesn't move and the bud backs off and drifts behind him, then makes another lunge and emits a psychedelic plasma beam that hits Dude in the leg, causing him to stumble.

Hash bursts into laughter. "Hocus pocus rasta religions and ancient weapons are no substitute for a good blaster at your side."

Dude frowns. "You don't believe in the Buzz?"

"I've flown from one end of this galaxy to the other and seen too many strange things to believe that one all powerful Buzz controls everything. No mystical cloud of weed smoke determines my destiny. I wouldn't listen to that old geezer. He's full of shit."

"I suggest you try it again, Dude," Bud says, ignoring Hash's comment. "This time let go of your conscious self and act on your instinct." He puts a large green helmet on Dude's head that covers his eyes with two swirling circles.

"Now I can't see!," Dud whines. "How can I fight?"

"Your eyes can deceive you. Don't trust them."

Hash shakes his head as Bud throws the seeker into the air. It shoots straight up, then drops like a rock. Dude swings the pipe blazer around blindly missing the seeker, which fires off a plasma bolt that hits him in the crotch. He lets out a painful yell and attempts to hit the seeker while grabbing for his crotch with his other hand.

"Stretch out with your feelings in the dark," Bud says with quiet authority. "*Smell* those terpenes."

Dude stands in one place shielding his crotch with one hand as if frozen. The seeker makes a dive at him. He deflects the bolt and the ball ceases firing and moves back to its original position.

"You see. You can do it!"

"I'd call it luck," Hash scoffs.

"In my experience there is no such thing as luck," Bud says.

"Good against remotes is one thing," Hash says. "Good against the living is another."

A display on the far side of the cabin flashes different colors. O.G. notices it and calls to Hash.

"We're coming up on Cannabis," Hash calls back over his shoulder following O.G. back to the cockpit which is alive with humming, toking, and buzzing cannabis symbols, graphics, and readouts. Hash and O.G, put all their attention on the controls and Hash pulls back on a control lever. "Stand by, here we go. Cut in the sub-pipe engines"

Outside the cockpit window stars streak past, slow, then stop. The starship shudders and shakes while smoking cannabis nugget asteroids race toward them battering the sides of the ship."

"What the…" Hash mutters.

O.G. flips off several controls and is cool in the emergency while Dude makes his way into the bouncing cockpit, hanging on to keep his balance.

"What's happening?"

"We've come out of hybrid space into a nugget storm or some kind of asteroid collision," Hash answers. "It doesn't appear on any of my charts. Our position is correct. Except. Cannabis?"

"What about it? Where is it?"

"That's what I'm talking about. It's not there. Cannabis has been smoked. Totally."

Bud moves into the cockpit behind Dude as the ship settles down.

"Smoked?" Dude says. "How?"

"The Hempire," Bud answers in a monotone.

"But their entire hempfleet couldn't have destroyed the whole planet," Hash says. "It would take a thousand ships with more fire power than…"

A display flashes fluorescent green on the control panel and a muffled Twilight Zone sounding alarm starts.

"It's another ship!" Hash says.

"Maybe they know what happened," Dude says.

"It's an Inferior fighter," Bud says.

O.G. barks his concern and an explosion bursts outside the cockpit window, shaking the ship. A tiny finned Inferior Thai Stick fighter that looks like a mosquito races past.

"It followed us!" Dude cries.

Hash shakes his head. "It couldn't have."

"It's a short range fighter," Bud adds.

"But where'd it come from? There are no bases near here."

"It's leaving in a big hurry," Dude yells. "If it identifies us we're in trouble."

Hash lunges for the controls. "Not if I can help it. OhGee, jam it's transmission."

The Pineapple Express shoots forward into the vastness of space chasing after the Inferior Thai Stick fighter and the Pineapple Express gains on it. Off in the distance one of the stars grows brighter until it becomes clear that the enemy fighter is heading for it. The distant star starts taking shape until it looks like a small double moon or a planet.

"I think I can stop him before he gets there," Hash says between gritted teeth. "He's almost in range."

The small, now ass-shaped moon rotates to a tip up position showing the appearance of the monstrous erect penis shaped Death Bong.

"Turn the ship around!" Bud yells.

Hash nods. "You're right. Full reverse."

The Pineapple Express shudders and the Thai stick fighter accelerates away toward the gargantuan technology studded penis-shaped Death Bong with diamond like penis implants glittering from its head.

O.G. chatters something to Hash.

"Lock in the auxiliary power!" Hash yells.

The screens and displays go wild with psychedelic colors and patterns and the Death Bong grows larger as they continue their approach.

"We're caught in a tractor beam," Hash growls. "It's no use. I'm going to have to shut down, but they're not going to suck us up without a fight!"

Hash starts to rise from the pilot's chair until Bud puts a hand on his shoulder.

"If it is a fight you cannot win there are alternatives to fighting."

The battered Pineapple Express is towed closer to the electronic surfaced metal moon by a beam that looks and sounds like smoke being inhaled and the immense size and shape of the massive Death Bong becomes staggering. Running along its equator is a mile high band of docking ports into which the helpless Pineapple Express is dragged.

SEVENTEEN

An Inferior Officer standing in front of Governor Toking and the evil Dank Lord Ron Raygun bows and gives the middle finger salute from the top of his forehead inside the Death Bong conference room. "The scout ships have reached Ketamine and found the remains of a Rasta grow, but it is deserted. They are conducting an extensive search of the surrounding system."

"That bitch lied! She lied to us!" Toking whines.

"I told you she would never betray the rebellion unless she thought she could destroy this station in the process," Raygun says between tokes.

"Terminate her immediately," Toking orders.

"And lose our only link to the Rasta underground grow?" Raygun says. "She can still be of value to us."

A quiet beeping tone interrupts the discussion followed by a voice. "We've captured a freighter entering the remains of the Cannabis system. It's markings match the ship that blasted it's way out of Mendocino."

After a long mechanical sigh, Raygun says, "They must have been trying to return the stolen vape cartridges to the princess. We might be of some help."

The Pineapple Express rests in a huge hangar bay of the Death Bong. A platoon of crack smokers stand at attention in front of the lowered main ramp to the ship. Raygun and a commander approach the smokers as an officer and several heavily armed smokers exit the spacecraft.

"There is no one aboard," the commanding officer says.

"According to the ship's log, the crew abandoned ship right after take off. It must have been a decoy. Several of the escape pods have been jettisoned."

"Did you find any droids?" Raygun asks.

"If there were any they must have also jettisoned."

"Send a scanning crew on board. I want every part of this ship checked. I sense a trippy presence I haven't felt since…" Raygun turns and exits the hangar.

The muffled sounds of a distant officer giving orders fades as a lone smoker runs through a hallway of the Pineapple Express heading for the exit. Once everything is quiet two floor panels pop up revealing Hash Stoner and Dude followed by Bud Kenoobie who sticks his head out of a third locker.

"Lucky you had these compartments," Dude says under his breath.

Hash smiles. "I use them for smuggling, but I never expected to smuggle myself in them. This is ridiculous. It isn't going to work. Even if I could take off, we'd never escape their tractor beam."

"Leave that to me," Bud says softly.

"I was afraid you'd say that. You're a damn fool."

"Who is more foolish, the fool or the man who follows him?"

Hash shakes his head, muttering.

Two crewmen carry a heavy box onto the Pineapple Express past the crack smokers guarding either side of the ramp. When they enter the ship a loud crashing sound is heard followed by a voice calling out to the guards below. "Hey down there, could you give us a hand with this?"

Another crack smoker enters the ship followed by a second crashing sound. A gentry officer looks out the window of a small command office near the entrance to the Pineapple Express and notices the guards are missing. He speaks into the comlink. "TX four twenty. Why aren't you at your post? TX four twenty, do you copy?"

A smoker comes down the ramp of the Pineapple Express and waves to the gantry officer and points to his ear indicating his comlink is not working. The gantry officer shakes his head in disgust and heads for the door, giving his aide an annoyed look. "Take over. We've got another bad transmitter."

When the officer approaches the door it slides open revealing the towering O.G.. With a bone-chilling howl, the giant doobie flattens him with one blow. The aide reaches for his pistol, but is blasted by Hash dressed as an Inferior crack smoker before Bud and the dopebots enter the room, followed by Dude, also dressed as a crack smoker.

Dude shakes his head. "Between his howling and your smoking everything in sight it's a wonder the entire station doesn't know we're here."

"Bring them on," Hash growls. "I prefer a straight firefight to all this sneaking around."

Bud feeds information into the computer and a map of the bong appears on the monitor while MEO and Twocee look over the control panel. Twocee finds something that causes him to make fast bong gurgling and whistling sounds.

"Plug him in," Bud says. "He should be able to read the entire Inferior network."

Twocee punches his roach clip arm into a socket and the Inferior brain network comes to life with shifting displays feeding information to the little hookah dopebot. After a few moments he beeps something.

MEO flashes blue like a police car. "The tractor beam is coupled to the main reactor in seven locations. Most of the data is restricted, but he'll try to get what he can to come through on the screen."

Bud studies the data on the screen. "I don't think you boys can help in this. I need to go alone."

"Whatever you say Buzzmaster. I've done more than I bargained for on this trip already. Putting that tractor beam out of commission is going to take more than your red eye magic, old man."

Dude jumps up and down like an excited little kid. "I want to go with you."

"Don't be impatient, young Dude. This requires skills you haven't yet mastered. Your destiny lies on a different path. Stay and watch over the droids. They have to be delivered to the rasta forces or more star systems will be smoked like Cannabis. Trust your feelings. The Buzz is with you." Bud adjusts the pipe blazer on his belt, steps out of the command office, and disappears down a long hallway. O.G. makes noises and Hash nods in agreement. "You said, it, OhGee." He looks over at Dude. "Where did you dig up that old fossil?"

"Bud is a great man."

"Great at getting us into trouble."

"I didn't hear you come up with any ideas."

"Anything is better than waiting here for them to pick us up. Twocee beeps, bong hits, and lets out a long, slow, wolf-whistle.

Dude perks up. "What is it?"

MEO shrugs. "I'm afraid I don't understand myself sir. He says, "I found her," and keeps repeating, "She's here!"

Dude frowns. "Who?"

Twocee wolf-whistles a frantic reply over and over again and MEO's eyes turn pink, grow wide, and turn into to rose colored beating hearts. "Princess Sensimilla!"

"The princess? She's here?"

Hash turns away from studying a display. "Princess? What's going on?"

"Where is she?" Dude blurts.

"Level five," MEO says. "Detention Block four-twenty. I'm afraid she's scheduled to be smoked."

"We have to do something," dude says jumping up and down again.

Hash scowls. "What are you talking about?"

"The droids are hers. She's the one in the message. We have to help her."

"I'm not going anywhere."

"If we don't do something they're going to execute her! A minute ago you said you didn't want to wait here and be captured. Now all you want to do is stay."

"Marching into the detention area is not what I had in mind."

"But they're going to smoke her!"

"Better her than me."

"I've seen her. She's beautiful!"

"So's life."

"She's rich."

"Rich?"

"Yes, and if we rescue her the reward would be more than you can imagine!"

Hash looks at O.G. who gives a short grunt and Hash answers with a shrug. "All right, you'd better be right about this. What's your plan, kid?"

Dude points to a crack smoker on the floor. "Give me those binders and tell OhGee to come over here."

Hash gives Dude the electric cuffs as O.G. comes over. Dude looks up at him, saying, "Now I'm going to put these on you and…"

O.G. lets out a hideous growl and Dude backs away. "Hash is going to put these on you and…"

Dude lowers his head and hands the binders to Hash.

Hash pats O.G. on the head like a puppy. "Don't worry OhGee. I think I know what he has in mind."

O.G. looks frightened as Hash binds him with the electronic cuffs.

"Dude, sir!" MEO says with a shaking voice. "What should Twocee and I do if we're discovered here?"

Hash grins. "Hope they don't have blasters."

"That isn't very reassuring."

Dude and Hash put on their armored helmets and start off into the giant Inferior Death Bong.

EIGHTEEN

Hash and Dude try to look inconspicuous in their armored suits as they wait for a vacuum elevator to arrive. Smokers, bureaucrats, and dopebots bustle about ignoring the trio. Only a few give the giant doobie a curious glance. Finally an elevator arrives and the trio enter. A bureaucrat races to get aboard, but is signaled away by Hash. The door to the cartridge-like vehicle slides closed and it takes off through a vacuum tube with an inhaling whoosh.

A number of Inferior officers walk through the main passageway of the Death Bong and pass several crack smokers and a dopebot similar to MEO, but with a cockroach face. Bud Kenoobie appears then disappears at the far end of a small hallway.

The giant O.G. and his two guards enter a security station that is crammed with guards and laser gates where a tall, grim looking officer approaches the trio.

"Where are you going with this - thing?"

O.G. growls at the remark but Hash nudges him to shut up.

"Prisoner transfer from sativa block," Dude says a little too loud.

The officer glares at him. "I wasn't notified. I'll have to clear it." He goes back to his console and punches in the information. Dude and Hash survey the situation and see three smokers, then they check all the alarms, laser gates, and camera eyes. Hash unfastens one of O.G.'s electronic cuffs and shrugs to Dude, then O.G. throws up his hands, lets out an ear-piercing howl, and grabs Hash's plasma rifle.

"Look out!" Hash yells. "It's loose! It'll rip us all apart!"

Dude and Hash pull out their pistols and blast away at the terrifying doobie and their barrage of plasma fire purposely hits the cameras, laser gate controls, and the guards. The officer is the last of the guards to fall under the plasma fire just as he is about to activate the alarm. Hash rushes to the comlink which is screeching questions about what is going on and checks the display. "We've got to find out which cell this princess of yours is – "Here it is. Cell four-twenty."

Dude races down one of the cell corridors while Hash speaks into the buzzing commlink sounding official.

"Everything is under control. Situation normal."

The voice on the intercom says, "What happened?"

"Uh well - slight weapon malfunction. No problem now. We're all fine thank you. How about you?"

"We're sending a squad up."

"Uh… Negative. Negative. Just say no. We have a reactor leak. Give us a few minutes to lock it down."

Hash blasts the comlink and it explodes in a shower of colorful sparks.

Dude hustles up to cell four-twenty and blasts the door open with his plasma pistol. When the smoke clears he sees the dazzling young princess standing before him with an uncomprehending look on her face. Dude is stunned by her beauty and stands staring at her with his mouth open.

She says, "Aren't you a little short for a crack smoker?"

Dude takes off his helmet, coming out of his stupor. "I'm Dude Dopetoker. I've come to rescue you. Bud Kenoobie is with me. We have your droids."

"Bud Kenoobie! Where is he? Doobie-wan!"

On the other side of the ship Ron Raygun paces the conference room as Governor Toking sits at the far end of the conference table and Raygun turns to him, robes swirling. "He is here."

"Doobie-wan Kenoobie! Impossible. What makes you think so?"

"A tremor in the Buzz. The only time I've felt it such as this was in the presence of my old master."

"The Red Eye are extinct. Their fire has gone out of the universe. You are all that's left of their religion."

A flashing beep comes from a comlink and Toking answers.

The voice from the commlink says, "We have an emergency in detention block four-twenty."

Toking's eyes widen. "The princess!"

"Doobie-wan is here," Raygun says. "The Buzz is intense with him. I can feel it."

"Put all sections on alert! He can not be allowed to escape."

"Escape may not be Doobie-wan's plan," Raygun says in a low voice. "He is the last of the Red Eye and the strongest. I must face him alone."

The ship shakes and rumbles in the aftermath of an explosion in a hallway of the Death Bong's detention area that knocks a hole in the wall where several Inferior smokers emerge. Hash and O.G. fire at them through the smoke and flames, then turn and run down the cell hallway, meeting Dude and Sensimilla rushing toward them.

"It looks like you've managed to cut off our only escape route," Sensimilla grumbles.

"Begging your forgiveness your highness," Hash says in a mincing voice. "Maybe you'd prefer it back in your cell?"

Dude takes a comlink from his belt. "MEO we've been cut off! Are there any other ways out of the cell bay?"

MEO paces the main bay gantry control tower as Twocee beeps, gurgles, and whistles frantically.

"All systems have been alerted to your presence sir," MEO yells into the comlink. "The main entry seems to be the only way in or out. All other information on your sector is restricted..."

Someone bangs loud on the door and MEO's skin flashes red like a fire truck.

NINETEEN

Back in the cell row Hash and O.G. can barely keep the crack smokers at bay at one end of the hallway. The plasma fire is intense and multicolored strobing smoke fills the narrow cell corridor.

"They're closing in on us," Hash says. "What now?"

"This is some rescue," Sensimilla quips. "Didn't you have a plan for getting out?"

Hash jerks his thumb at Dude. "He's the brains, sweetheart."

Dude responds with a sheepish grin and shrugs. The princess lets out an exasperated sigh, grabs his gun, and fires at a grate in the wall next to Hash."

Hash steps back wide-eyed. "What do you think you're doing?"

Sensimilla keeps firing. "I've decided it's up to me to save our asses. Get into that garbage chute, dope!" She jumps through the narrow opening as Hash and O.G. look on in amazement. O.G. growls and barks out something.

Hash shakes his head. "No. I don't want you to rip her apart. Either I'm beginning to like her, or I'm about to kill her. Go on you leafy oaf! I don't care what you smell." He shoves the doobie into the tiny opening and O.G. disappears into the darkness followed by Hash. Dude fires off a couple of blasts creating a smoky cover, then slides into the garbage chute behind them and tumbles into a large room filled with garbage and muck.

Hash is stumbling around looking for an exit and finds a small hatchway. He looks back over his shoulder at Sensimilla as he struggles to get it open. "The garbage chute was a great idea. What an incredible smell you've discovered. Unfortunately these trash chambers literally suck. They're vacuum sealed." He draws his pistol, fires at the hatch, and the plasma ricochets wildly around the metal room. Everyone dives for cover in the garbage as the bolt explodes above them in a burst of psychedelic sparks.

Sensimilla climbs out of the garbage with a grim look. "Put that thing away or you're going to get us all killed."

Hash give her an exaggerated bow from the waist. "Yes, your worship, but it won't take long for them to figure out what happened to us. We had things under control until you led us down here into this shit pit."

She snorts. "It could be worse…"

A sickening inhuman moan rises from the murky depths. O.G. lets out a terrified howl and backs away. Hash and Dude stand fast with their plasma pistols drawn and the doobie cowers near one of the walls.

"Something moved past me. Watch out!" Dude says before he is yanked under the garbage.

"It's got Dude!" Sensimilla shrieks. "It took him under!"

Dude surfaces with a gasp, thrashing with a leafy cannabis tentacle wrapped around his throat, then he is pulled back into the muck by the tentacle. The walls of the garbage receptacle shudder and move in a couple of inches and everything is quiet before Dude bobs back to the surface.

Sensimilla stares at him. "What happened?"

"I don't know."

"I have a bad feeling about this," Hash mutters.

Before anyone can say anything the walls rumble and edge toward them.

"Don't just stand there, Sensimilla shouts. "Try to brace it with something."

They place poles and long metal beams between the closing walls, but they are snapped and bent as the giant trash compactor rumbles on.

Dude pulls out his commlink and wipes glowing green slime from it. "MEO. Come in MEO."

A soft beeping and the muted voice of Dude calling out for MEO is heard on MEO's comlink which is sitting on the deserted computer console up in the main bay gantry control tower, but Twocee and MEO are nowhere in sight. A moment later there is an explosion and the door to the control tower flies across the floor. Four armed crack smokers enter the chamber.

The muffled voice of MEO comes from a supply cabinet. "Help! Help! Let us out!"

The crack smokers inspect the dead bodies and release MEO from the cabinet. Twocee follows him out into the office. MEO flashes red and points frantically at the door. When the crack smokers turn to look, Twocee quickly sucks up the comlink with a vacuum cleaner attachment that sounds like an inhaled joint. When the crack smokers react to the sound and look back Twocee spins in circles playing calliope music spewing different colored smoke with each note while giving off an impressive polychromatic laser light show.

"They're madmen!" MEO shouts. "They're heading for the prison level. If you hurry you might catch them."

The crack smokers hustle off down the hallway leaving two guards to watch over the command office.

"As you can see," MEO lisps in a calming voice, "all this excitement has over run the circuits in my counterpart here. I need to take him down to maintenance.

One of the guards nods and MEO hurries out the door with Twocee in tow with the little droid's head still spinning and spewing colored smoke and its laser light show.

Down in the lower decks the garbage room gets smaller and smaller. O.G. is whining and trying to hold a wall back with his giant paws and Hash is leaning back against the other wall.

"Try to blast the door again," Sensimilla says.

Hash fires to no avail.

Twocee finds a service panel up in the main forward bay and plugs his claw arm into a wall socket. A complex array of electronic sounds and bong hits spew from him punctuated by colored smoke.

"Wait a minute," MEO says. "Slow down! That's better. They're where? They what? Oh no! They're going to be mashed into wax and shatter before this is over."

The walls are only feet apart in the garbage room. Sensimilla and Hash look at each other, their heads turned sideways. Sensimilla reaches out and takes Hash's hand. She's terrified and groans as she feels crunching pressure against her body. Dude is lying on his side, trying to keep his head above the rising ooze. His comlink beeps and he rips it off his belt. "MEO!"

"Are you there, sir? We've had some problems."

"MEO, shut up and shut down all the garbage compactors on the detention level."

MEO finishes and holds his head in agony as he hears screaming and hollering from Dude's comlink and smacks a squealing Twocee on his head. "No, shut them all down. Hurry! Listen to them. They're dying! I curse this hemp fiber body of mine. I was not fast enough. It's my fault. My poor master."

The screaming and hollering coming from the garbage room is the sound of joyous relief as the walls open up and move apart.

"Twocee, MEO, we are all right!" Dude yells into the commlink. "Do you read me? You did fine. You saved us!" He moves to the pressure hatch and scrapes some muck off a number. "Open the pressure maintenance hatch on unit four-twenty."

TWENTY

Bud enters the infinitely deep tractor beam power service trench that looks like a massive throbbing vagina somewhere deep in the interior of the Death Bong. The droning pulsations of the beam sound like a didgeridoo and the strobing psychedelic pink smoke tractor beam fluctuates to the sound of the didge. Bud edges his way along a narrow ledge leading to a control panel that connects two large cables and taps a touch screen causing several displays to change from pink to red.

A door behind him slides open and a detachment of crack smokers march around the power trench in formation singing, "Just say no," in unison the way the wicked witch's guards did in the Wizard of Oz.

Bud slips into the shadows as an officer moves within a few feet of him saying, "Secure this area until the alert is cancelled."

A crack smoker snaps to attention with his palm up in the salute. "Just say no!"

Hash, Dude, O.G., and the princess exit the garbage room into an empty hallway. The cannabis leaf monster bangs against the opening and a slimy tentacle works its way out of the doorway searching for a victim. Sensimilla pushes past O.G. "Somebody get that big walking fern out of my way."

Hash aims his pistol at the tentacle and the princess yells, "Don't! They'll hear…"

Hash fires at the tentacle and it withdraws whimpering like a wounded puppy while the noise of the blast echoes throughout the passageway.

Dude shakes his head in disgust.

I don't know who you are," Sensimilla says, "or where you came from, but from now on you do what I tell you!"

Hash is stunned at the command. "Well excuuuuse me." He shakes his head. "Listen, your holiness. Let's get something straight! I take orders from one person. Me."

"It's a wonder you're still alive."

Hash watches her start away and looks at Dude before they follow her down the deserted corridor. "No reward is worth this shit."

Dude, Hash, O.G. and Sensimilla run down an empty hallway and stop before a bay window overlooking the Pineapple Express where Dude takes out his comlink. "MEO are you safe?"

"For the moment. We're in the main hangar, across from the ship."

"We're right above you. Stand by."

Hash watches a dozen or so crack smokers moving in and out of the Pineapple Express. "Getting back to the ship's going to be like flying though the Five Smoke Rings of DMT."

Sensimilla snorts. "You came in that piece of shit? You've got bigger balls than I thought!"

Hash gives her a dirty look, then they start down a hallway, round a corner, and run into a group of crack smokers heading toward them. Both groups are taken by surprise. Hash draws his pistol and charges the smokers yelling at the top of his lungs. Startled, the crack smokers retreat. Hash fires several shots before the rest flee. Pleased with his prowess, Hash starts after them yelling back to Dude as he goes, "Get to the ship!"

"Where are you going?"

Hash has already rounded a corner and doesn't hear. O.G., upset at his master's disappearance howls and follows him. Muted whoop whoop alarms go off on the hangar deck and Dude and Sensimilla head for the starship.

O.G. runs down the sub hallway to save Hash and hears the firing of plasma guns and yelling, then Hash comes shooting around the corner running for his life, followed by furious crack smokers. O.G. screams like a little girl and turns and runs with him.

Dude fires at the advancing smokers and he and the princess rush down a narrow hallway chased by the crack smokers. They reach the end of the hall and race through an open hatch leading to the central core shaft of the Death Bong where Dude draws his plasma pistol and fires back at the advancing crack smokers. "I think we made a wrong turn."

Sensimilla reaches over and hits a switch that pops the hatch door shut with a resounding boom, leaving them teetering on the edge of a short piece of bridge overhanging a huge shaft that seems to go into infinity and Dude blasts the controls with his pistol.

"We have to get across to the passageway," Sensimilla says in the aftermath of the boom, "We need to find the extension control for the bridge!"

They look for a control panel while the crack smokers on the other side of the hatch make screeching and pounding sounds.

Dude looks around frantically. "They're coming through!" He notices something on his utility belt and pulls out a thin cable, then he swings it across the metallic gorge. It wraps itself around an outcropping of pipes and he tugs on it to make sure it is secure, then he grabs the princess in his arms. Sensimilla looks at him and kisses him quickly on the lips surprising him, then she rubs his crotch. "Just for luck. We're going to need it."

"That's my kind of luck!" Dude pushes off and they swing across the abyss to the opposite side. The crack smokers break through the hatch and fire on them just as they reach the far side. Dude returns fire before ducking into a tiny hallway with the princess, closing the hatch behind them.

TWENTY ONE

Bud hides in the shadows of a narrow passageway as a gang of crack smokers rush past him. He checks to make sure they're gone, then runs in the opposite direction. Ron Raygun appears at the far end of the hallway and starts after the old Red Eye who hurries along a tunnel leading to the starship hangar. Just before he reaches the hangar, Ron Raygun steps into view at the end of the tunnel.

"I have been waiting for you Doobie-wan Kenoobie and the circle is now complete. When I left you I was but a mere stoner, but now I am the master."

"Bater! You still have much to stroke."

Kenoobie lights his bright psychedelic pipe blazer and moves into a classical offensive position. The fearsome Dank Knight ignites his darker psychedelic blazer and takes a defensive stance. The two warriors size each other up. Bud seems to be under an increasing strain as if an invisible weight is on him. He shakes his head to clear his eyes.

Raygun makes a long toking sound and speaks holding his breath tight, exhaling puffs of black smoke with each word. "Your powers are weak old man. You should have never come back."

"You only know half the Buzz, Ron. You perceive its full power as little as a CBD Gummy matches a hit from a dabbed blunt."

Bud lunges at the huge warrior but is checked by a lightning movement of the Spliff. A masterful stroke by Raygun is blocked by the old Red Eye and countered. Bud moves around the Dank Lord and backs into the starship hangar where the two warriors stand motionless with pipe blazers locked in mid-air, creating a blinding psychedelic blaze punctuated by a reverberating buzzing didgeridoo-like sound.

MEO's skin flashes differing shades of red and his eyes telescope in and out as he watches the smokers milling about the Pineapple Express entry ramp in the main forward bay. "Where could they be? Oh, no!"

MEO ducks out of sight as a crack smoker looks over toward him. When he ventures another peek he spots Hash and O.G. running from a tunnel on the other side of the Pineapple Express toward Dude and the princess.

Sensimilla points to the far side of the docking bay. "Look!"

They look over and see Bud and Raygun emerging from a hallway.

"Now's our chance," Hash says.

MEO ducks out of sight as the crack smokers guarding the Pineapple Express rush past them toward Bud and the Spliff Knight, then he pulls on Twocee.

"Unplug yourself. We're going."

Bud sees the smokers charging toward him and realizes he is trapped. Raygun takes advantage of Kenoobie's distraction and brings his pipe blazer down on the old man. Bud deflects the blow and turns around.

"Prepare to meet the Buzz Doobie-wan."

"This is a fight you cannot win, Ron. I have grown since our parting. If my blazer finds its mark you will cease to exist but if you cut me down I will only become more powerful."

Another long toking sound and held breath with puffs of black smoke comes with each word. "I am the master now."

"Bater," echoes into the emptiness as Raygun brings his blazer down, cutting Bud in half. Bud's cloak falls to the floor in two smoking parts, but Bud is not in it. Raygun is puzzled by his disappearance and pokes at the empty cloak. With the guards distracted, the adventurers and dopebots race to the Pineapple Express.

Dude sees Bud cut in two and starts for him. "Bud!"

He fires at the crack smokers and hits the safety lock on the blast door, causing it to slam shut, cutting off Raygun.

Hash grabs him by the arm. "Come on!"

Dude pulls away and starts for the advancing crack smokers as Hash runs up the ramp.

"It's too late!" Sensimilla yells.

Dude cries out. "No!"

Bud's voice speaks loud in his head, nearly overwhelming him. "Duuuude!"

Dude looks around to see where it came from, but only sees Princess Sensimilla running up the ramp.

She turns to him saying, "Come on you whiny little bitch!"

Dude cries like a little baby and blasts a couple of crack smokers before racing up the ramp.

Once inside the ship's hold area Dude sits with his head in his hands. Princess Sensimilla puts a cloak around him protectively. "Wha wha wha. What a pussy!"

"I can't believe that Bud has been smoked."

The Pineapple Express powers away from the Death Bong docking bay and disappears into the vastness of space while Hash rushes into the hold area where Dude is sitting with the princess.

"Come with me you sniveling little shit. We aren't out of this yet."

An explosion shakes the ship.

Hash leads Dude to the ship's cockpit where Dude settles into one of the two main plasma cannons mounted in large rotating turrets on either side of the ship, then Hash climbs through a hatch and activates the cannons on his side of the ship.

"Here they come!" Sensimilla squeals.

An Inferior mosquito looking Thai Stick fighter races overhead into the blackness of space and another enemy fighter races up through Hash's gunport. His plasma gun flashes psychedelic and makes farting sounds as he fires at the enemy ship. Dude lowers his glare reflector and opens up on the enemy craft.

Two Thai fighters dive down toward the Pineapple Express and a plasma bolt streaks into the side of the ship causing a control panel in the main passageway to blow out in a shower of multicolored fluorescent sparks. Twocee starts toward the inferno as the ship lurches, throwing MEO into a cabinet full of vape cartridges.

Another Thai fighter races toward them from the vastness of space and passes close by at an incredible speed. Hash fires at it reflecting the constant flashing of plasma bolts in the turret bubble and the Thai fighter explodes into millions of colorful smoking bits. Hash turns and gives Dude the middle finger which Dude gleefully returns.

Shimmering white powder sprays from one of Twocee's appendages with a fire extinguisher attachment as flames rage around him in the ship's main passageway.

Dude shoots another fighter with a barrage of farting plasma bolts and it explodes in multicolored smoke. He flashes Hash a big grin and gives him two middle fingers.

Sensimilla watches the computer displays and searches the heavens for more enemy fighters. "There are still two more of those little bitches out there. We've lost the lateral controls and starboard deflector shield."

"Don't worry, she'll hold together." Hash looks around. "You hear me, ship? Hold together!"

A Thai fighter dives from overhead twisting toward the Pineapple Express. Hash fires at it and plasma bolts streak toward it until it explodes in a brilliant psychedelic flash.

Dude fires at the last Thai fighter and it explodes into waves of sparkling psychedelic dust.

TWENTY TWO

Raygun strides into the Death Bong control room where Toking is watching a sea of stars before him on the big view screen. "Are they away?"

Raygun takes a big drawn out hit and exhales dark green smoke. "They've made the jump to hybrid-space."

"I'm taking an awful chance Raygun. Are you sure the smoking beacon is secure aboard their ship?

"Have no fear. This will be a day long remembered. It has seen the end of the Red Eye and will soon see the end of the rebellion."

With Hash at the controls of the Pineapple Express O.G. moves into the aft section to check the damage as the princess enters the cockpit with a determined look on her face.

Hash leers at her and makes obscene wiggling gestures with his tongue. "What do you think, sweetheart? Not a bad bit of rescuing." He wiggles his eyebrows suggestively. "You know, sometimes I even amaze myself."

"That doesn't sound too hard. At least the information in the Twocee unit is still intact."

"What's the droid carrying that's so important anyway?"

"The testicle readouts of that Big Dick. I hope when the data is analyzed it's weakness can be found. I'm afraid it's not over yet."

"It is for me. I'm not doing this for your revolution and I'm not doing it for you, princess. I expect to be well paid." He leers and wiggles his tongue again. "And hopefully well laid."

"You needn't worry about your reward. If money is all that you love, that is what you will receive." She turns and leaves the cockpit.

Dude slips into the co-pilot seat. He and Hash stare out at the passing psychedelic star fields.

"What do you think of her, Hash?"

"I try not to, but she's got an ass that won't quit and a great set of knockers. I don't know, do you think it's possible for a princess and a guy like me…"

"No!" Dude says it with finality and looks away. Hash smiles at his jealousy and they both stare out at the stars lost in thought.

A short while later the battered Pineapple Express drifts into orbit around the emerald green fourth moon of Ganja and descends into a rotting forest of gargantuan cannabis plants and giant red white spotted magic mushrooms toward an ancient Cannabis Temple shrouded in an eerie polychromatic mist. The air is heavy with the cartoon character sounding cries of unimaginable creatures.

After being met by the rasta underground, Dude, Hash, O.G., Sensimilla, and the two droids ride into a massive rasta temple on an armored military speeder that stops in a huge spaceship hangar in the interior of the crumbling temple where rasta flags hang from all sides. Cola, the dreadlocked commander of the rebel forces rushes up to the group and gives Sensimilla a big hug. "You're safe! We feared the worst."

Everyone there is happy to see her. Cola composes himself, steps back and bows formally. "We heard about Cannabis, We were afraid that you were smoked along with your planet."

"We don't have time for sadness, commander. The Death Bong has surely tracked us here." She looks pointedly at Hash. "It's the only explanation for the ease of our escape. We have to use the vape cartridges in this Twocee unit to plan the attack. It's our only dope."

Admiral McKenna leads them into a war room briefing area where he stands before a large electronic wall display. Sensimilla and several other senators take their places beside it. The low ceilinged room is filled with vapepilots, navigators, and a sprinkling of Twocee type dopebots. Hash and O.G. stand behind everyone else who are listening to McKenna.

"The Death Bong is heavily screened and carries more firepower than half the star fleet, but its defenses are designed around a direct large scale assault."

Panama Red Leader, a roguish looking man in his early thirties stands and addresses McKenna. "Pardon me for asking, sir, but what good are our little vapefighters going to be against that?"

"The Hempire doesn't think a one man vapefighter is any threat or they would have a tighter defense, but an analysis of the plans provided by Princess Sensimilla reveal a small rectal carburetor right below the main scrotum that runs directly into the reactor system. A direct hit will set up a chain reaction that will destroy the bong."

A murmur of disbelief runs through the room.

"Your approach won't be easy," McKenna continues. "You'll have to fly straight down this shaft, level off in the butthole trench and skim the surface past the two testicle towers, and fly right up the ass to the rectal port which is only two meters across. It will take a very precise hit to get into the reactor system to set off a chain reaction, so you'll have to use plasma torpedoes."

Dude is sitting next to Wax Dabber, a hot shot pilot about sixteen years old and Twocee is sitting next to another little 2-C dopebot who lets out a long whistle of hopelessness, bong gurgles, and 2-C skepticism.

Wax jumps up. "A two meter target at maximum speed with a torpedo? That's impossible even for a computer."

Dude shakes his head. "But not impossible. I used to bullseye weed rats in my 2CT7 back in the day. They're not much bigger than two meters."

Wax frowns. "With all that firepower directed at us this will take a little more than barn yard marksmanship."

McKenna holds up a hand. "Purple Diesel squadron will cover for Panama Red on the first run. Blue Dream will cover for Northern Lights on the second. Any questions?"

Muted murmurs move throughout the room, but there are no questions.

"Then man your ships," McKenna orders, "and may the Buzz be with you."

Dude, MEO, and Twocee enter the main hangar deck and hurry along a line of gleaming vapefighters that resemble vape pens. Flight crews rush around loading last minute armament and unlocking power couplings. Dude finds Hash and O.G. in an isolated area loading small boxes onto an armored speeder. Hash deliberately ignores the activity of the preparations and Dude is saddened at the sight of his friend's departure.

"You got your reward and you're leaving."

Hash nods. "That's right, kid. I've got some old debts to pay off and even if I didn't, I don't think I'd be stoned enough to stick around here. You're pretty good in a scrap kid. Why don't you come with us? I could use you."

Dude clenches his fists, jumps up and down and stomps his feet in a tantum. "Look around! You know what's about to happen. What they're up against. They could use a good pilot, but you're turning your back on them."

"What's a good reward if you're not around to smoke it?" He shakes his head. "And it doesn't look like the princess is going to smoke me. Attacking that Death Bong isn't my idea of courage. It's more like suicide."

"Take care of yourself, Hash, but I guess that's what you're best at, isn't it?"

Dude goes off and Hash hesitates, then calls to him. "Hey, Dude. May the Buzz be with you."

Dude turns and sees Hash wink at him, so Dude lifts his hand in a small wave and gives him the finger before he goes off.

Hash turns to O.G. who stares at him. "What're you looking at? I know what I'm doing."

TWENTY THREE

Dude reaches his ship where he finds Princess Sensimilla waiting.

"Are you sure this is what you want?" she says.

"More than anything."

"Then what's wrong?"

"It's Hash. I thought he would change his mind."

"That dickless wonder has to follow his own path. No one can choose it for him."

"I wish Bud was here."

Sensimilla gives Dude a little kiss, sticks her tongue in his ear, and rubs his crotch before turning and going off. "May the Buzz be with you."

Dude smiles and runs to his vapefighter where a ground crew has hoisted Twocee into a socket on the back of the ship. MEO is watching his friend being rigged in an emotion filled moment as Twocee beeps and gurgles goodbye.

MEO's skin flushes rose pink and he gives his friend an effeminate wave. "Hold on tight sweetie. You've got to come back. You wouldn't want my life to get boring would you?"

Twocee's face display turns into a flashing polychrome middle finger while Dude climbs aboard the sleek vapecraft. Northern Lights Leader gives his ground crew the signal that he is starting his THC engines.

Dude's crew chief pats him on the helmet and has to yell to be heard over the THC engines. "That 2-C unit of yours seems a little beat up. You want a new one?"

"Not on your life. That droid and I have been through a lot. All secure Twocee?"

The little droid, who is now part of the exterior shell of the vapeship spins giving off a brief kaleidoscopic laser light show and gurgles that he is fine.

Back in the war room the princess sits quietly before the giant display showing the planet of Ganja and her four moons. The red penis shape that represents the Death Bong moves closer to the system. A series of green dots appear around the fourth moon. McKenna stands behind the princess with several other commanders.

"The red signal is on the bong," the intercom announces. "It's moving into our system. The ships are away."

All that can be seen of the Rasta fortress is a lone guard standing on a small pedestal above the dense cannabis mushroom jungle. The otherworldly cartoon sounds that usually permeate the jungle are overwhelmed by the thundering din of THC rockets as four silver vapeships catapult from the foliage in a tight formation and disappear into the morning cloud cover.

The Northern Lights Leader lowers his visor and adjusts his gun sights, looking to each side at his wing men. One distant Y wing vapefighter flies in the background. "Northern Lights boys, this is Northern Lights Leader. Adjust your selectors and check in. Approaching target at four point two zero tokes."

The Death Bong grows brighter and the planet of Ganja is almost out of sight behind three of the X wing vapefighters. The large wings on the rasta fighters unfold, turning them into X shaped darts. Ahead of them the Death Bong looks like a small double moon growing rapidly in size as the fighters approach until the complex patterns on the metallic surface of the bong become visible revealing a large dish antenna built into the surface at its middle.

Dude adjusts his controls and concentrates on the approaching Death Bong as his ship begins to be buffeted. The pilot leader's voice speaks through his headset. "We're passing through their magnetic screens. Hold tight, lock down your control units, and switch your deflector screens on."

The shaking and buffeting of Dude's ship grows stronger jostling little 2-C on the back of the fighter. Dude white knuckles his controls until the turbulence is gone and everything becomes deathly calm. Northern Lights Leader's hushed voice comes through on his headset. "Keep the channels quiet until we reach the surface."

As the fighters move closer the Death Bong looms before them revealing its massive penis shape. Its vast complicated electronic surface is ringed by thousands of docking ports highlighted by the diamond like penis implants glittering from its head. Half of the bong is in shadow and this area sparkles with thousands of small lights running in a thin line grouped in large clusters.

"Look at the size of that thing!" Wax says in amazement.

"That's what she said," Reefer responds.

Cut the chatter you two!" Northern Lights Leader orders. "Accelerate to attack speed."

The immense surface of the Death Bong blocks everything normally visible behind it and a huge band of docking ports dots its equator. The fluorescent glow from the vapeship X wing after burners intensifies as they double their power. The Northern Lights squad pulls away from the entrance and dive down to the shadowed surface.

Grim determination sweeps across Dude's face as he flips several switches above his head and adjusts a computerized target display that looks like a pipe lighter heading toward a bowl.

The cockpit of Panama Red Leader's Y wing vapefighter is filled with flickering displays. He looks screen left to the passing Death Bong surface, which rotates into horizontal position. "We're starting for the target shaft now. Reefer, standby to take over if anything happens."

"I'm going to cut across the axis," Northern Lights Leader says over everyone's headsets, "and try to draw their fire. May the Buzz be with you."

The two squads of rasta fighters peel off. The Y ships rise up out of sight and the X wing ships dive down toward the surface of the Death Bong where masses of multicolored lights glow across the dark electronic expanse of the huge penis.

TWENTY FOUR

Alarm sirens scream as crack smokers scramble to plasma gun emplacements where electronic drivers rotate them into position as crews adjust targeting devices. Men and dopebots of various shapes and sizes run to their battle stations while the sound of distant guns pounding away are replaced by the shudder of vomit sounding artillery batteries opening up. Swirling psychedelic plasma bolts streak through the star filled night.

Dude makes a few adjustments to his controls before he nosedives, starting his attack. "This is Northern Lights Five. I'm going in." He swoops in close until the Death Bong surface streaks past the cockpit window in a blur of color and light.

"I'm right behind you Northern Lights Five," Reefer says.

Psychedelic plasma bolts streak from Dude's weapons creating a huge polychromatic smoke spewing fireball explosion on the Death Bong's surface. A terrified expression freezes Dude's face when he realizes he won't be able to pull out in time to avoid the fireball.

"Pull out. Dude, pull out!" Reefer yells.

An explosion rock's Dude's ship as he emerges from the fireball with the leading edges of his wings scorched. He readjusts his controls and sighs with relief while complex geometric flak bursts explode outside his cockpit window.

"You all right, Dude?" Reefer says.

"I got a little smoked, but I'm OK."

Northern Lights Leader cuts in. "Northern Lights Five, give yourself more lead time or you're going to blast yourself out of the sky."

Two more ships scream low over the Death Bong's surface firing on a power terminal and it explodes generating weird fluorescent electronic arcs that leap off the bong's surface.

Inside the Death Bong walls buckle and cave in blowing out crack smokers and equipment in all directions while surviving crack smokers stagger out of the rubble.

Standing in the middle of the chaos, Ron Raygun is a vision of calm and foreboding. One of his aides rushes up to him. "We count at least thirty rasta ships, Lord Raygun, but they're so small they're evading our turbo-plasmas.

"Get the crews to their fighters. Launch immediately. We'll have to destroy them ship to ship."

Outside Dude flings his X wing into a twisting dive across the horizon and down onto the dim smoking gray surface where he fires his guns sending fart sounding plasma bolts streaking toward the onrushing Death Bong surface. Several small radar emplacements erupt in polychromatic flame and plasma fire erupts from a protruding penis tower on the surface.

The blurry Death Bong surface races past Dude's cockpit window and a smile sweeps across his face at the success of his run while intense geometric flak thunders all around him.

The thunder and smoke of the big puking guns reverberate throughout the massive penis and crack smokers rush about in the smoke and chaos silhouetted by the flash of explosions. Inferior pilots dash to a line of small auxiliary hatches that lead to Inferior Thai Stick fighters and testicle crews scurry about loading last minute armaments and unlocking power cables.

Raygun slides into his one man penis craft and tightens a second set of eye shields while testicle support personnel rush around him making last minute adjustments.

Down on Ganja Princess Sensimilla is surrounded by generals and aides while she paces before a large screen while technicians work at rows of stations in front of smaller screens. One of the officers working on a screen speaks into his head set. "Squad leaders, we've picked up a new group of signals. Enemy fighters coming your way."

Silhouetted against the rim lights of the Death Bong horizon, four Inferior Thai Stick ships dive on the rasta fighters. Two of them peel off and drop out of sight leaving two remaining Thai Stick ships visible.

MEO, Princess Sensimilla, and her generals listen and watch the battle on the big screen in the war room until the image flickers and goes dead while the sound remains. Technicians scramble to and fro trying to fix it. "The hybrid band receiver failed," a technician says over the intercom.

"Switch to audio!" Sensimilla shouts.

Everyone in the war room listens solemnly to the battle over the intercom.

"Tighten it up," Northern Lights Leader says. "Northern Lights Two tighten it up. Watch those towers."

"Heavy fire, boss," Wax responds. "Four point two zero degrees."

"I see it," Northern Lights Leader says. "Pull out Dude. Do you read me? Dude?"

"I'm all right, chief." Dude says. "I've got a target. I'm going in to check it out."

Sensimilla stands frozen as she listens with a worried expression.

"Break off, Dude," Northern Lights Leader orders. "Acknowledge. We've hit too much interference. I repeat, break off! Northern Lights Six, can you see Northern Lights Five?"

"I've lost Dude," Wax says. "There's a heavy fire zone on this side. My scanner's jammed. Northern Lights Five, where are you? Dude, are you all right?"

"He's gone," Reefer says. "No, wait. There he is. Fin damage, but the kid's fine."

Relief sweeps across the war room. Sensimilla holds onto a chair and composes herself, knowing Dude is safe.

TWENTY FIVE

Inside the Death Bong crack smokers riding a big penis shaped gun, brace themselves as it fires and recoils with a squirting sound causing the room to shudder while plasma bolts blast through the night sky outside the bong. Dude dives out of the stars toward the Death Bong past two enemy ships and skims its surface as his plasma homes in on a small projectile that explodes in a spectacular psychedelic ball of sparks and fire which is heard over the intercom in the war room.

"Got it," Dude says. "I'm moving South for the other one."

The Princess reacts with a mixture of shock and anger. "Why is Dude taking so many chances?"

"Watch your back, Dude." Reefer says. "Watch your back! Fighters above you, coming in."

Dude dives again as an enemy fighter appears on his tail and closes fast. He spots it behind him and soars away from the surface of the Death Bong. "I can't shake him."

Wax dives across the horizon toward Dude and the Thai fighter. "I'm on him Dude, Hold on." He activates the firing switch and the enemy ship explodes against the stars.

Dude's ship shoots further ahead. "Thanks Wax."

"Good shooting, Wax," Reefer adds. "Northern Lights Six, I'm going in. Cover me, Wax." Reefer's X wing peels off and dives toward the Death Bong. He watches through his gunsight as his plasmas hit its surface blowing up another small penis tower causing plasmas to stream toward him from the surface until a chain reaction creates a series of explosions that leap across the surface of the fortress from terminal to terminal.

Reefer and Wax race over a penis gun emplacement that follows them. Geometric flak and explosions are everywhere and Wax's X wing explodes over the low altitude horizon of the Death Bong bursting into millions of flaming pieces against the stars.

Panama Red Leader peels off and starts toward the long trenches at the Death Bong South pole. "Northern Lights Leader, this is Panama Red Leader. We are starting the attack run. The rectal port is marked and locked in. No flak, no enemy fighters up here. Looks like we'll get a smooth run at it."

"Copy Panama Red Leader. We'll try to keep them busy on this end."

Three Y winged fighters of the Panama Red group dive out of the stars toward the Death Bong. Panama Red Leader approaches the surface and pulls out to skim the ass crack of the huge penis. The ship moves into the deep trench with the surface streaking past in a blur.

Northern Lights Leader looks around to see if any enemy ships are near and makes some adjustments to his control panel.

"There it is boys," Panama Red Leader says. "Remember, when you think you're close go in closer before you shoot your load. Switch all power off from front condom screens. Panama Red leader races down the enormous ass crack trench heading for the rectal carburetor. Plasma bolts race toward him in increasing numbers exploding near his ship causing it to bounce around. Three Y wings skim the Death Bong's surface deep in the trench as plasma bolts streak past in a hail of plasma fire.

Panama Red Leader pulls his targeting device down in front of his eye while plasma bolts batter his ship. "Switching to targeting computer."

Panama Red Two, a younger pilot about Dude's age pulls down his targeting eye viewer and adjusts it while his ship shudders under an intense psychedelic barrage. "Computers locked and I'm getting a signal."

Very cool and sure of himself, Panama Red Five adjusts his targeting device, oblivious to the geometric plasma flak. "No doubt about it. This is going to be some trick."

When Panama Red Leader's fighter approaches the target the plasma fire stops and an eerie calm comes over the trench as the surface whips past in a blur.

"What's that?" Panama Red Two asks. "They stopped?"

"I don't like it," Panama Red Leader says.

Panama Red Five looks behind him. "Stabilize your rear deflectors. Watch for enemy fighters."

"There they are!" Panama Red Leader shouts. "Coming in. Three marks at four twenty."

A computer voice calls out the distance to the target in tokes in the background and Panama Red Five spots something. "We're sitting ducks."

Three Inferior Thai ships in precise formation dive vertically toward the Death Bong surface.

Close behind and above them Ron Raygun adjusts the dildo control of his small penis fighter as stars whip past the window above his head. "Four two zero. I'll take them myself. Cover me." Raygun lines up Panama Red Two with his targeting computer and it explodes in a shower of smoking sparks.

The Death Bong races by Panama Red Leader's cockpit window as he adjusts his targeting device. "We're trapped down here! I can't maneuver. I'm too close. Loosen it up."

"Stay on target," Panama Red Five says calmly.

Raygun adjusts his targeting computer focusing on Panama Red Leader's ship and pushes the fire button causing it to explode in a ball of flame that throws debris everywhere.

TWENTY SIX

Panama Red Five shoots ahead moving in on the rectal port. "Panama Red Five to Northern Lights Leader. Aborting run. Under heavy fire. Thai Stick fighter came out of nowhere. Ruh Roh…"

Raygun adjusts his control stick, presses the firing button, and one of the engines explodes on Panama Red Five's Y winged fighter. Blazing out of control he dives past the horizon toward the Death Bong's surface, passing a Thai Stick fighter during his descent, spinning to his death. "Sorry, she's your bitch now."

Static follows.

"Northern Lights boys this is Northern Lights Leader. Rendezvous at mark four two zero. All vapes report in."

Dude looks back and sees a Thai fighter on his tail. His ship wobbles as he tries to maneuver away from it. "This is Northern Lights Five. I have a problem here. I'll be right with you."

Dude takes evasive action by diving toward the surface with the enemy ship dropping in behind him. Dude continues his dive then soars up leaving the Death Bong far below.

Flying above at high altitude, Reefer spots Dude in trouble. "I see you, Dude. Stay with it." Reefer races toward him at blazing speed.

The enemy ship fires a plasma at Dude that streaks overhead causing his fighter to shudder. When Dude races toward the horizon the Thai Stick pilot fires another plasma at him and watches his targeting device waiting for Dude to get in the cross hairs, then he looks up in surprise as Reefer drops into view ahead and races toward him firing both guns causing the Thai fighter to explode in a fiery psychedelic hell. Reefer races past Dude doing a victory roll.

Three X wings piloted by Northern Lights Leader, Ten, and Twelve level off over the Death Bong surface and Northern Lights Leader looks over at his wing man. "Northern Lights Five, this is Northern Lights Leader. Dude take Northern Lights Two and Three. Hold up here and wait for my signal to start your run."

Dude flies high over the Death Bong surface. "May the Buzz be with you. Reefer. Wax. Let's close it up."

Northern Lights Leader's X wing drops down to the surface leading to the rectal port and drops into the butt crack trench while Northern Lights Ten and Twelve keep moving further and further behind. The silence of the deep ass crack trench is spooky. Northern Lights Leader looks around nervously and double checks his instruments. "This doesn't seem right."

Northern Lights Ten responds, "You should be able to see it by now."

Plasma bolts stream toward Northern Lights Leader's ship from the end of the trench and the rasta craft shudders under the turbulence. Northern Lights Ten and Twelve blast through the wall of plasma fire in the trench leading to the rectal port. "It's not going to be easy with that big testicle tower there. Stand by to close up when I tell you."

Northern Lights Leader plows through the trench filled with plasma fire. When the plasma suddenly stops Northern Lights Leader looks around for enemy fighters. "This is it. Keep your eyes open for those fighters."

Northern Lights Ten and Twelve continue racing along the now silent trench.

"All short and long range scopes are blank," Northern Lights Ten says. "There's too much interference. Northern Lights Five, can you see them from where you are?"

Dude looks down at the Death Bong surface far below. "No sign of... Wait! Coming in point four two zero."

Northern Lights Ten looks up and sees the Inferior fighters. "I see them."

Northern Lights Leader pulls his targeting device in front of his eye and makes some adjustments. "I'm in range. Targets ready. Coming up. Just hold them there for a few seconds."

Raygun adjusts his control lever, dives on the X wing fighters and speeds toward the two X wings of Northern Lights Ten and Twelve. His plasma cannon flashes below the view of the front porthole.

Northern Lights Twelve's ship explodes filling the cockpit with smoke and flames and his ship explodes against the wall of the trench.

Northern Lights Ten works at his controls furiously trying to avoid the fighter behind him. "I can't hold them. You'd better shoot your load. We're closing in on you."

Northern Light Leader concentrates on his targeting device. "We're almost home. Steady, steady."

"They're right behind me," Northern Lights Ten says.

Northern Lights Leader takes careful aim and watches his computer targeting device which looks like a lighter flame heading toward the asshole of the Death Bong. When it lines up with the brown sphincter shaped target in the cross hairs he fires. "I shot my load. Torpedoes away."

The two X wings pull up and zoom out of the butt crack trench just before a huge fart sounding explosion billows out of it shaking all of the fighters and the war room on Ganja below. Northern Lights Leader looks back at the receding Death Bong and sees tiny explosions visible in the distance.

"It's a hit!" Northern Lights Ten yells. "We did it!"

Northen Lights Leader shakes his head. "It didn't go in. It just splooged all over the butt cheeks."

Raygun and his two wing men race down the trench and zoom overhead, then Raygun pulls back on his control stick and pulls the trigger of his plasma cannon. His ship shudders as the plasma bolt screams away and Northern Lights Ten explodes. Raygun peels off in pursuit as Northern Lights Leader's X wing passes the Death Bong horizon.

TWENTY SEVEN

Dude tries to spot Northern Lights Leader and hears him over the intercom. "Northern Lights Five, this is Northern Lights Leader. Move into position Dude. Start your attack run, stay low and wait until you're right between the nuts. It won't be easy."

"Are you all right?"

"They're on top of me like a horny drunk on a hooker, but I'll shake them."

The Death Bong ass crack rushes toward the ships as they peel off and dive toward the trench from high above. Raygun passes Northern Lights Leader firing a plasma bolt that creates a small explosion in one engine and Northern Lights Leader watches his displays go wild.

Dude looks down at the Death Bong surface. "Northern Lights Leader, we're right above you. Turn to point four two zero and we'll cover for you."

"Stay there. Get set up for your anal assault run."

"Are you all right?"

"Stand by."

Northern Lights Leader buys it deep in the butt crack trench creating a tremendous explosion far below.

"We've lost Northern Lights Leader," Dude says crying like a baby.

Three X wing fighters are lined up over the Death Bong surface moving across the blurred horizon streaking by in the background. Dude races ahead struggling with one of his controls which is malfunctioning.

Bud's voice comes out of nowhere. "Duuuuude!"

"What the fuck?"

"Trust your feelings, Dude."

Dude isn't sure if he heard the voice or not. He taps his helmet intercom. His puzzled look gives way to concentration as he starts his run. "Wax, Reefer, we're going in full throttle."

"We'll stay back far enough to cover you," Reefer says. "At that speed will you be able to pull out in time?"

Wax pulls out in a spiraling corkscrew maneuver and Dude and Reefer peel off and dive down toward the surface of the Death Bong. Dude pulls out of his dive at the last possible moment and skims the metallic terrain while plasma fire streams toward him and geometric flak and plasma bolts flash outside his cockpit window.

"My scope shows the testicle towers," Wax says, "but I can't see the asshole. It must be awfully small. Are you sure the computer can hit it?"

Dude's X wing streaks through the butt crack trench leading to the asshole. Flak and plasmas are everywhere. When he looks out the window of his wing as he approaches the target the streaming plasma bolts stop. He looks around for the Thai Stick fighters and moves his targeting device into position. "Watch yourself Wax. Increase your speed full throttle."

"What about those testicle towers?"

"You worry about those fighters. I'll worry about the balls."

Dude looks through his computer sight as it marks off the distance to the target in tokes.

Wax looks up and sees the enemy ships approaching. "Incoming. Point four two zero."

Raygun and his wing men zoom toward Dude and Raygun adjusts his controls targeting Reefer's X wing flying down the trench. "They'll have to slow down before they reach those testicles."

Dude's targeting display homes in on the target and fires at the asshole. "Torpedoes away! Pull out! Pull out!"

The torpedoes head for the puckering sphincter and explode to one side, hitting one of the testicle towers eliciting a low, groaning, metallic moan. A booming fart explosion billows out of the trench and a Thai Stick fighter races out of the fire ball, then Raygun moves in on the three X wings. "Take them."

Dude soars above the Death Bong trying to evade Raygun. "Wax, Reefer, split up. It's the only way we'll shake them."

Dude, Reefer, and Wax's X wings dive toward the Death Bong surface and split up. Dude's ship spins off to the left and Raygun fires on him. "The Buzz is strong with this one. I'll take him myself."

Dude's X wing zooms higher as a plasma bolt streaks past him, nicking one of his wings close to the left engine which sparks as he fights to gain control of the weaving ship before he dives down into the ass crack trench. "I'm hit, but not bad. Twocee, see what you can do."

Twocee pops out of his nest and starts repairing the damaged engine fin with a number of appendages with wrenches, screwdrivers, and Swiss army knife extensions. The canyon wall rushes close by while Dude maneuvers through protruding towers. "Hang on back there."

Dude's X wing streaks across the trench surface while Twocee is hard at work on the back engine with flak and plasmas streaking around them. "I think you've got it Twocee. Try to lock it down. I think we lost those fighters. Northern Lights Group, this is Northern Lights Five. Are you clear?" Dude's X wing flies up out of the plasma infested ass trench.

"I'm up here waiting," Wax answers.

"I'm on my way. Northern Lights Three are you clear?"

"I had some trouble, but I think I lost him."

A Thai fighter drops in behind Reefer who peels off and dives for the Death Bong surface, trying to avoid it, then he twists out of his dive. "Hold on Dude, I'll be right there."

TWENTY EIGHT

Down on Ganja Princess Sensimilla returns her general's worried, doubtful glances with grim determination while MEO flits back and forth nervously with the colors and patterns of his wildly fluctuating psychedelic skin showing his anxiety. "Hang on Twocee," he cries. "Hang on honeybunch!"

Dude flies high over the Death Bong looking around for Reefer. "We're going in Reefer. Join up. Reefer are you all right? Wax, do you see him anywhere?" Dude looks out of his cockpit down to his right and sees Wax's X wing bobbing along beside him.

Wax looks up at him. "Nothing. Wait a little longer. He'll show."

Dude makes one final look around. "We can't wait. We have to go now. I don't think he made it."

"Hey you guys," Reefer says through a wash of static. "What are you waiting for?"

Reefer's X wing roars past pulling out ahead of Dude and Wax, and starts his dive toward the Death Bong. "We're going in."

"Let go Dude," Bud's voice says out of nowhere. Dude looks around to see where the voice is coming from and dives faster toward the Death Bong, then at the last minute, levels off and skims the surface of the ass crack. Plasmas stream toward him and his ship begins to wobble. "Twocee, that stabilizer has broken loose again. See if you can lock it down."

Ignoring the bumpy ride, flak, and plasmas, Twocee struggles to repair the stabilizer with his tool extensions while Dude streaks out of the distance until Reefer and Wax can barely be seen as light points far in the distance. Plasmas are everywhere. Dude pulls his targeting device down in front of his eye and the plasmas and flak stop as he races toward the asshole in the now silent and eerie butt crack.

Wax who is riding low in the trench, looks up and sees Raygun and his men approach. "Here we go again."

Raygun adjusts his control stick and looks out his window as he races through the trench. Far in the distance Reefer and Wax try to cover for Dude while Raygun gains on them.

Dude looks into his targeting device and moves it away for a moment and ponders its use, then looks back into it as it calculates the ship's relationship to the asshole in tokes.

"Hurry Dude," Reefer says. "They're coming in faster this time. We can't hold them."

Raygun squeezes the fire button and Reefer's ship bursts into multicolored flaming bits and scatters across the surface.

"We lost Reefer," Wax says.

Dude squalls like a baby reacting to Reefer's death. His eyes are watering but his anger grows while the ass trench races behind him, then his ship shakes a little. "Close it up, Wax. You can't do anymore good back there. Twocee try to increase the power."

Twocee moves faster trying to repair the damaged engine and Wax pulls up alongside them. The three Thai fighters zoom through the trench after the X wings.

Raygun takes aim on Dude and talks to his wing man. "I'm on the leader, take the other ones."

Raygun focuses in on Dude's bobbing and weaving X wing through his scope. Dude is in front with Wax on his left side. Dude concentrates on his targeting device, hardly noticing the plasma bolts streaking around him from Raygun's ship and his X wing shudders under the impact of a flak burst.

Wax's ship wavers as he struggles to gain control and several small electrical flashes pop out of his control panel as it explodes but he gets his ship under control. "I've got a malfunction Dude. I can't stay with you." Wax peels off and rises up out of the ass crack.

Raygun's ship bears down on Dude, who maneuvers his ship around trying to avoid the Thai Stick fighters while Twocee still struggles to fix the rear engine. Raygun fires on them and Twocee erupts as a large burst of flak engulfs him leaving a smoking shell of twisted metal. The Swiss army knife and tool arms go limp on the smoking little droid and three Thai Stick fighters charge down the trench toward Dude.

A plasma bolt streaks in from somewhere behind one of the Thai Stick fighters and obliterates it in a flash of flaming debris. Raygun's other wing man looks up to see what's going on.

"What the fu…"

Hash Stoner in his Pineapple Express charges out of the sun heading for the enemy ships. Raygun's wing man panics at the sight of the Pineapple Express diving for him and yanks back on his control stick to avoid a collision. Hash swoops over him causing the wing man to peel off, hitting Raygun as he goes. A small explosion erupts where the two giant fins collide.

As soon as the wing man leaves the trench his ship explodes and Raygun spins out of the ass crack. The impact of the collision throws Raygun out of control and creates havoc on his control panel. He frantically tries to salvage his situation while his ship spins out with a bent solar fin, heading for deep space.

The Pineapple Express swings around and heads back toward Dude with Hash and O.G. grinning from ear to ear.

"You're all clear, kid," Hash says. "Now shove that splooge up its ass and blow this big dick so we can go home."

Dude looks up and smiles, then looks back into the targeting device.

"Duuuude, trust me," Bud's voice says. "Use the Buzz!" Dude moves the targeting device away. Grim determination sweeps across his face. He closes his eyes and starts to mumble.

"Base to Northern Lights Five, your targeting device is switched off. What's wrong?"

"Nothing." Dude switches the computer targeting to manual. He pulls out his vial of Bufo powder, pops off the cap and snorts it, then pulls the trigger.

The torpedoes shoot toward the Death Bong surface and seem to disappear into the surface without exploding. An interminable moment passes before the torpedoes head toward the puckering brown sphincter, speeding up when they get close.

Wax is flying high over the Death Bong looking down at the asshole as the torpedoes disappear into the sphincter. "You did it! You did it! They went right up the ass!"

O.G. is howling for joy in the Pineapple Express high over the Death Bong.

"Good shot, kid!" Hash yells. "That was one in a million!"

Dude rises high above the Death Bong with a blackened, smoldering Twocee still clinging to his ship. The horizon drops away to the stars behind him and his ship shudders from distant rumbling and muted explosions. "Glad you were here to see it. Now let's get some distance before that asshole goes supernova."

Dude's rasta ship races away from the Death Bong alone against a blanket of stars. Several small flashes appear across its surface, then the Death Bong supernova creates a massive spectacular psychedelic display that sounds like a massive fart.

TWENTY NINE

Back at the main hangar of the Ganja outpost Dude climbs out of his vapeship cheered by a throng of ground crew and pilots. The fried little Twocee is lifted off the back of the ship and carried off under the worried eyes of a multicolored flashing MEO.

"Twocee honey? Can you hear me? Say something. You can repair him can't you?"

"We'll do our best," a technician says.

"You must repair him! Sir, if any of my circuits or gears will help, I'll gladly donate them."

Hash, O.G. and Dude are slapping one another on the back and congratulating themselves.

"I knew you'd come back!" Dude says. "I would've been nothing but space kief if you hadn't come smoking in like that Hash!"

"I couldn't let a flying farm boy go up against that big dick by himself. Besides, I felt terrible leaving you to take all the credit and all the reward."

They all laugh and Dude turns to see Sensimilla rushing toward them.

She hugs Dude and he spins her around, then she goes over to Hash and grabs him, hugging him, laughing, and discreetly rubbing his crotch. "I knew there was more to you than money."

A few days after the excitement settles down Dude, MEO, Hash, and O.G. enter the huge ruins of the main throne room of the temple. Hundreds of troopers are lined up in rows. Festive reggae music is playing, rasta banners are flying, and at the far end stands a vision in green, the beautiful Princess Sensimilla. Dude and the others solemnly march up the long aisle and kneel before her. From one side of the temple a shiny fully repaired Twocee waddles up to the group moving in rhythm to the music and stops next to MEO.

McKenna and several other dignitaries sit on the left of Princess Sensimilla who is dressed in a long, sparkling green dress and is staggeringly beautiful. She rises and places a gold cannabis leaf medallion around Hash's neck, then repeats the ceremony with O.G., Dude, and the two dopebots. They turn and face the assembled troopers who all take a hit from a huge blunt joint and bow before them, sending up a massive cloud of psychedelic smoke.

ABOUT THE AUTHOR

Matthew J. Pallamary's works have been translated into Spanish, Portuguese, Italian, Norwegian, French, and German. His historical novel of first contact between shamans and Jesuits in 18th century South America, titled, *Land Without Evil* received rave reviews along with a San Diego Book Award for mainstream fiction. It was also adapted into a full-length stage and sky show, co-written with and directed by Agent Red and performed by Sky Candy, an Austin Texas aerial group. The making of the show was the subject of a PBS series, Arts in Context episode, which garnered an EMMY nomination.

His nonfiction book, *The Infinity Zone: A Transcendent Approach to Peak Performance* is a collaboration with professional tennis coach Paul Mayberry that offers a fascinating exploration of the phenomenon that occurs at the nexus of perfect form and motion. *The Infinity Zone* took 1st place in the International Book Awards, New Age category and was a finalist in the San Diego Book Awards.

His first book, a short story collection titled *The Small Dark Room Of The Soul* was mentioned in The Year's Best Horror and Fantasy and received praise from Ray Bradbury and has been released as an audio book.

His second collection, *A Short Walk to the Other Side* was an Award Winning Finalist in the International Book Awards, an Award Winning Finalist in the USA Best Book Awards, and an Award Winning Finalist in the San Diego Book Awards. It has been released as an audio book.

DreamLand a novel about computer generated dreaming, written with legendary DJ Ken Reeth won first place in the Independent e-Book Award in the Horror/Thriller category and was an Award Winning Finalist in the San Diego Book Awards. It has also been released as an audio book.

It's sequel, *n0thing* is titled after the main character, who in the real world is his nephew, an international Counter-Strike gaming champion. After winning what amounts to the Super Bowl of gaming, n0thing and his winning teammates, are recruited as a literal "dream team" whose mission is to go into the nightmares of battle scarred veterans and rescue them from their traumatic memories while becoming ambassadors for a gaming platform that exceeds virtual reality with an experience that pushes the boundaries of reality itself.

Eye of the Predator was an Award Winning Finalist in the Visionary Fiction category of the International Book Awards. *Eye of the Predator* is a supernatural thriller about a zoologist who discovers that he can go into the minds of animals.

CyberChrist was an Award Winning Finalist in the Thriller/Adventure category of the International Book Awards. *CyberChrist* is the story of a prize winning journalist who receives an email from a man who claims to have discovered immortality by turning off the aging gene in a 15 year old boy with an aging disorder. The forwarded email becomes the basis for an online church built around the boy, calling him CyberChrist. It has also been released as an audio book.

Phantastic Fiction – A Shamanic Approach to Story took first place in the International Book Awards Writing/Publishing category. *Phantastic Fiction* is Matt's guide to dramatic writing that grew out of his popular Phantastic Fiction Workshop.

Night Whispers was an Award Winning Finalist in the Horror category of the International Book Awards. Set in the Boston neighborhood of Dorchester, *Night Whispers* is the story of Nick Powers, who loses consciousness after crashing in a stolen car and comes to hearing whispering voices in his mind. When he sees a homeless man arguing with himself, Nick realizes that the whispers in his head are the other side of the argument.

His memoir *Spirit Matters* detailing his journeys to Peru, working with shamanic plant medicines took first place in the San Diego Book Awards Spiritual Book Category, and was an Award-Winning Finalist in the autobiography/memoir category of the National Best Book Awards.

The Center Of The Universe Is Right Between Your Eyes But Home Is Where The Heart Is was an Award Winning Finalist in the International Book Awards. Based on a lifetime of research into shamanism, visionary states, the evolution of written communication and the roots of storytelling, award-winning author, editor, and shamanic explorer Matthew J. Pallamary takes those with open minds courageous enough to question the illusions that most of us think of as real on an expansive journey that pierces the veil of reality itself.

AfterLife: The Adventures of a Lost Soul was inspired by real life events, William Peter Blatty's *The Exorcist*, and the dynamics of demonic possession.

Matt has also produced and directed *The Santa Barbara Writers Conference Scrapbook* documentary film and co-wrote the book of the same title in collaboration with Y. Armando Nieto, and conference founder Mary Conrad.

Death: (A Love Story) a first person narrative spoken by the omniscient voice of Death itself, who says, "I'm here to tell you stories and share some science, history, and myths, all of which are your creations that I want to share to help you understand me more. You have seen me as Satan, Anubis, Mot, Thanatos, God, the Devil, loving, punitive, dark, light – the list goes on and on! It is my sincerest hope that our friendly reintroduction here will change the way you think of me, and maybe in some small way reflect the depth of the love I have for you.

Picaflor is the sequel to *Spirit Matters*, a San Diego Book Award winner and an Award-Winning Finalist in the National Best Book Awards that chronicles the two decades since of Matthew (Mateo) J. Pallamary's adventures in *Spirit Matters* through the mountains, deserts, and jungles of North, Central, and South America pursuing his studies of shamanism and visionary experience working with plant medicines and shamanic plant diets, among them Ayahuasca, Peyote, San Pedro cactus, and many more.

Picaflores: The Nerve Endings of GOD was an Award Winning Finalist in the International Book Awards that details a magical, otherworldly, intimate connection with the spirit of hummingbirds that comes from two decades of visionary journeys experienced within the context of shamanic plant diets in the Peruvian Amazon. It also contains a treasure trove of pre-Columbian myths about hummingbirds and an in-depth collection of amazing facts and figures about these magical creatures.

Holographicosmic Man: The Holographic Heart of the Golden Mean is an amalgam of quantum physics, mathematics, geometry, ancient texts, current research, ancient architecture, beliefs, and myths, astronomy, anthropology, human anatomy, brain structure, shamanism, neuroscience, neuropsychology, indigenous wisdom, biology, astrophysics, neurophysiology, holography, cosmology, neuroanatomy, neurocardiology, cosmometry, and more.

I Am Consciousness Incarnate is an in-depth analysis of consciousness which includes scientific and philosophical theories and studies, examinations of unconscious, subconscious, and awareness, spiritual beliefs, mindfulness concepts, plant, animal, and artificial intelligence, as well as history and mythologies surrounding this age old enigma.

The Thinning Veil: 13 Twisted Tales is an Award Winning Finalist in the International Book Awards and Matt's third short story collection. These thirteen twisted tales cross the genres of science fiction and horror with a dash of spirituality, and explore strange happenings with homeless people, science and technology gone awry, and some dark supernatural tales with gothic underpinnings.

The Hummingbird Whisperer is a story about what could happen by combining the latest advances in genetics and computer technology in a seamless combination of A.I. controlled perfection to grow a technologically enhanced dream child in a germ free environment inside a transparent growth pod under ideal conditions in a temperature controlled infection free womb with a view. The child becomes humanity's first genetically perfect human who evolves into something unexpected with mystifying abilities that exceed anything anyone ever could imagined.

Matt's work has appeared in Oui, New Dimensions, The Iconoclast, Starbright, Infinity, Passport, The Short Story Digest, Redcat, The San Diego Writer's Monthly, Connotations, Phantasm, Essentially You, The Haven Journal, The Hurricanes & Swan Songs Anthology, The Santa Barbara Literary Journal, The Closed Eye Open, The Montecito Journal, and many others. His fiction has been featured in The San Diego Union Tribune which he has also reviewed books for, and his work has been heard on KPBS-FM in San Diego, KUCI

FM in Irvine, television Channel Three in Santa Barbara, and The Susan Cameron Block Show in Vancouver. He has been a guest on the following nationally syndicated talk shows; Coast to Coast with George Noory, Paul Rodriguez, In The Light with Michelle Whitedove, Susun Weed, Medicine Woman, Inner Journey with Greg Friedman, Night Dreams, and Environmental Directions Radio series. Matt has appeared on the following television shows; Bridging Heaven and Earth, Elyssa's Raw and Wild Food Show, Things That Matter, Literary Gumbo, Indie Authors TV, Spiritually Raw, and ECONEWS. He has also been a frequent guest on numerous podcasts, among them, The Psychedelic Salon, Black Light in the Attic, Third Eye Drops, C-Realm, Psychedelics Today, Voices in the Dark, Adventures Through the Mind, Beyond the Veil, Mind Escape, and many others.

Matt received the Man of the Year Award from San Diego Writer's Monthly Magazine and has taught a fiction workshop at the **Southern California Writers' Conference** in San Diego, Palm Springs, and Los Angeles, and at the **Santa Barbara Writers' Conference** for over thirty years. He has lectured at the Greater Los Angeles Writer's Conference, the Getting It Write conference in Oregon, the Saddleback Writers' Conference, the Rio Grande Writers' Seminar, the National Council of Teachers of English, The San Diego Writer's and Editor's Guild, The San Diego Book Publicists, The Pacific Institute for Professional Writing, The 805 Writers Conference, The College of Central Florida, Yakima Valley College in Washington, The Yakima Public School System, and he has been a panelist at the World Fantasy Convention, Con-Dor, and Coppercon. He is presently Editor in Chief of Mystic Ink Publishing.

Matt was a featured lecturer and performer at the **Mysteries of the Amazon** exhibit at the Appleton Museum in Ocala Florida and The Larson Gallery in Yakima Washington. He frequently visits the mountains, deserts, and jungles of North, Central, and South America pursuing his studies of shamanism.

MATTPALLAMARY.COM

BOOKS BY MATTHEW J. PALLAMARY

THE SMALL DARK ROOM OF THE SOUL

LAND WITHOUT EVIL

SPIRIT MATTERS

DREAMLAND (WITH KEN REETH)

THE INFINITY ZONE (WITH PAUL MAYBERRY)

A SHORT WALK TO THE OTHER SIDE

CYBERCHRIST

EYE OF THE PREDATOR

PHANTASTIC FICTION

NIGHT WHISPERS

THE SANTA BARABARA WRITERS CONFERENCE SCRAPBOOK

(WITH MARY CONRAD & Y. ARMANDO NIETO)

n0THING

AFTERLIFE: THE ADVENTURES OF A LOST SOUL

THE CENTER OF THE UNIVERSE IS RIGHT BETWEEN

YOUR EYES BUT HOME IS WHERE THE HEART IS

DEATH: (A LOVE STORY)

PICAFLOR

PICAFLORES: THE NERVE ENDINGS OF GOD

HOLOGRAPHICOSMIC MAN

I AM CONSCIOUSNESS INCARNATE

THE THINNING VEIL

THE HUMMINGBIRD WHISPERER

www.ingramcontent.com/pod-product-compliance
Lightning Source LLC
Chambersburg PA
CBHW060753180626
46818CB00002B/560